ACCLAIM FOR
THE FIVE SEASONS OF LOVE

Four seasons, then a fifth – João Almino's novel is a love song to life. Surrounded by memorable friends, his lucid protagonist, Ana, takes up the wisdom and courage of middle age, the joy to be found on the other side of failure and loss. With deftness and passion, Almino spells out the momentous promise of deep friendship between men and women. For him it is the seed of a new season for us all.

– Mary Louise Pratt
  Professor of Comparative Literature, New York University

Almino's novel offers the true force of literary experience: literature is thought in action; literature is philosophy that does not stop thinking.

– João Cézar de Castro-Rocha, University of Manchester

This is a novel of intensities, of passionate encounters, both for the narrator and the reader; of places that you will recognize, enjoy, and sometimes even begin to hate, although you may have never seen them. Above all, this is a novel of the certainty that pervades all passion and all places, the certainty that Love, could it ever be achieved at all, or endure forever, would be the redemption and perhaps even the transfiguration of our existence. Seen from these Five Seasons of Love, *João Almino's trajectory as a novelist seems to convey, in a compressed version, the history of the novel over the past century: having gone through many levels of formal experimentation, having engaged in multiple strategies to productively provoke his readers, he is now a powerful presence in what we might call the 'existentialist turn' of the genre. This novel is about the 'World' again, about the defining impossibility of women and men to find a stable place in the World; and it does so with tones and in colors that are neither loud nor bitter. If you manage to read João Almino sympathetically, if you are able to engage with the existence of Ana, his beautiful protagonist and narrator, then this novel will convince you that we must live - and should try to live happily - with the minimal opportunities ~~*~~ life has to offer.*

– Hans Ulrich Gumbrecht

member of the American Academy of Arts & Sciences

Love and friendship, Brasília and its dreams of the future, and the unexpected workings of time and desire are the subjects João Almino investigates in The Five Seasons Of Love. *This is a fascinating novel, wise and full of news, and no one interested in contemporary Brazil should miss reading it.*

— David Beaty, writer

This new and extraordinary novel by João Almino redefines the Brazilian nation as something that was to be invented by humankind.

— Silviano Santiago, writer and literary critic

At times reminiscent of the concise psychological realism of Graciliano Ramos while occasionally echoing Clarice Lispector's characters undergoing precious and painful moments of epiphany, João Almino's The Five Seasons of Love *courageously portrays the physical albeit imaginary trope of Brasília as a site of trans-formation, in every sense of the word.* The Five Seasons Of Love *is a novel where characters embark on transitions that transcend the prison of the past to arrive at new beginnings and personal renewal. Through these pages, the reader is treated to the dynamics of trans-formative movement on all levels humanly possible: the geographic, the societal, the political, the psychological, the emotional, the spiritual, and even the sexual. This is a novel that movingly and compellingly illustrates a theory of the "trans" in formation.*

— Dr. Steven F. Butterman, University of Miami

The Five Seasons of Love *pits the right-angled Brasília of Niemeyer and Costa's plan against a humanity prone to twists, turns, and zigzags against any conceivable plan or grid. The result is a polychrome Brasília (and a Brazil) far richer, more engaging and deeply human than the dreams of architects and social engineers.*

— Jeffrey Schnapp, Director, Stanford Humanities Lab

THE FIVE SEASONS OF LOVE

JOÃO ALMINO

TRANSLATED FROM THE PORTUGUESE BY
ELIZABETH JACKSON

WITH AN INTRODUCTION BY
K. DAVID JACKSON

HOST PUBLICATIONS
AUSTIN, TX

Host Publications, 277 Broadway, Suite 210, New York, NY 10007

Layout and Design: Joe Bratcher & Anand Ramaswamy
Cover Photo: Anand Ramaswamy
Jacket Design: Anand Ramaswamy

First Edition

Library of Congress Cataloging-in-Publication Data

Almino, João.
  [Cinco estações do amor]
  The five seasons of love / Joao Almino ; translated from the Portuguese
by Elizabeth Jackson ; with an introduction by K. David Jackson.
     p. cm.
  ISBN-13: 978-0-924047-50-3 (hardcover : alk. paper)
  ISBN-10: 0-924047-50-X (hardcover : alk. paper)
  ISBN-13: 978-0-924047-51-0 (pbk. : alk. paper)
  ISBN-10: 0-924047-51-8 (pbk. : alk. paper)
  I. Jackson, Elizabeth. II. Title. III. Title: 5 seasons of love.
  PQ9698.1.L58C5613 2007
  869.3'4--dc22
                              2007041176

ACKNOWLEDGEMENTS

I am grateful to Professor David Jackson, of Yale University, who first drew attention to this book in the U.S., by organizing a symposium on "The Five Seasons of Contemporary Brazilian Fiction" and by including *The Five Seasons of Love* in one of his courses. I am mostly indebted to Elizabeth Jackson for her initiative, dedication and a competent, excellent translation. I thank my publishers Joe W. Bratcher, III and Elzbieta Szoka, of Host Publications, for enthusiastically embracing the project. My gratitude also to my friends Charles Perrone, Chris Peterson and Maria Louise Phillips for their encouragement and advice. Most of all, I thank my wife Bia Wouk. I dedicate this book to her, with whom I have spent the best seasons of love.

INTRODUCTION

WRITING THE FUTURISTIC CITY:
BRASÍLIA'S *FIVE SEASONS OF LOVE*

The great cities of the world have a special relationship firmly established with the modern narrative. World cities have been brought to life by classic narratives vitally related to what distinguishes them, especially the great European capitals, whether Dublin's Joyce, Prague's Kafka, Paris's Proust, Berlin's Döblin, or London's Woolf. The Tate Modern's current exhibition "Global Cities" (2007) expands far beyond Europe to include the largest and most dynamic cities on all continents. Brazil, the world's fifth largest country in area, has seen rapid urbanization, and its capital, Brasília, seems to have literally materialized out of nothing on the country's central plateau, without any literature and only a series of notes in the historical record.

When Brasília was inaugurated on April 21, 1960, the city was the most audaciously futuristic ever designed and constructed as a national capital. There were no inhabitants and no roads. It could only be reached by airplane, and its palaces, ministries, and "superblocks" of residences seemed as strange as a brave new world. It was designed in the shape of a cross, or some say an airplane, and all its streets were one-way with no intersections. Street lamps used fluorescent lighting. In that same year, Simone de Beauvoir found Brasília to be an artificial city in the middle of a desert; she wrote about the recently inaugurated capital, "I'm leaving Brasília with the greatest pleasure...this city will never have a soul, heart, flesh or blood."[1] One of Brazil's greatest writers, Clarice Lispector, was already fascinated by the city in 1962 when she wrote: "Brasília is artificial, as artificial as the world must have been when it was created... Construction with space calculated for clouds."[2]

The architect Oscar Niemeyer's "Statement"[3] about planning the city shows that function gave rise to form. It was a project of high modernism, and function was primarily aesthetic and symbolic: useful structures would be capable of transmitting "beauty and emotion" permanently. Niemeyer described the challenge he faced as being the need to reconcile total freedom for the imagination with a unique character for both buildings and the overall design. Yet his novel design disguises within Brasília's radical futurism the ghost of great world cities and their designs and development in history: the High Court was meant to have the "sobriety of the great squares of Europe" and the great concave and convex chambers of the National Congress were meant to realize Le Corbusier's ideal of "correct and magnificent volumes assembled in light." In his book on the city in history, Lewis Mumford cites one of the vulnerabilities of the planned city, from Versailles to Washington, D.C., Canberra to Chandigarh, which is form without function. Whether composed of monumental Baroque façades, broad avenues, or geometrical designs, the planned city is not designed to change over time. It is the material realization of a pure idea, an architectural concept in which the useful or practical is a function of aesthetic design and form.

Brasília, the futuristic capital city of Brazil, was officially opened by President Juscelino Kubitschek when it could be reached only by air or horseback. Brasília thus began its still brief existence as a paradox. It was planned as a vanguard of modern architecture where form and functionality would recast political and urban life in a planned and controlled space of aesthetic grandeur, where the individual would be minimized by the spatial grandiosity and the open horizons of the central plateau. Brasília opened as the mythical city of the New World, absent any human or social character, a space without any narrative of its own, as unoccupied as blank pages waiting for characteristic inscriptions that would in time allow it to join the other great capitals with a narrative space of its own. Its mythical dimension allowed André Malraux to see in it already "a resurrection of the architectural lyricism born in the Hellenic world," and he called it "the capital of hope." It seemed to him the "first capital of a new civilization" and "the most audacious city the West ever conceived."[5]

Brasília in its futuristic incarnation of 1960 was the ghostly presence and unfulfilled form of a long-standing architectonic and geo-utopian dream of a capital city in the interior, and author João Almino reviews the notable historical references to a long-nurtured desire to build a new capital in the interior in a retrospective essay.[6] In the early nineteenth century, both the independence movement in Minas Gerais and the 1817 revolutionaries in Pernambuco defended the idea of establishing a national capital in the interior on the central plateau. Nationalist politician Hipólito José da Costa, exiled in London in 1808, placed the future capital at the head of great rivers in the interior, whereas the actual placement of Brasília would correspond by an uncanny coincidence with a suggestion of José Bonifácio de Andrade e Silva in 1821, before the declaration of independence, that the future capital be located at approximately fifteen degrees latitude and that it be called "Petrópole, Brasília or some other name." The historian and diplomat Francisco Varnhagen suggested in 1849 that countries with capital cities in the interior have greater culture, wealth, and population through the promotion of communication, commerce, agriculture, and industry. According to Tomás Coelho in 1877, a capital on the high plain would represent a locus of authority from which orders would "descend," irradiating to the far corners of Brazil. Legal proposals to move the capital began in 1852 and continued through the constitutions of 1891, 1934, and 1946, followed by technical studies for its precise location. A foundation stone to mark a possible location of the future capital was laid on September 7, 1922, on the centenary of Brazil's independence. The definitive location was chosen on April 15, 1955, and during construction the stone from 1922 was located within the actual Federal District.

Brazil's great author Machado de Assis, in a newspaper column on January 22, 1893, saw the inevitability of a new capital and expressed his hope that it would gain its own population right away and that it would be habitable. Here the great writer put his finger on perhaps the main and most persistent doubt that is still present in the Brazilian mind as regards Brasília: who are the permanent residents and how do they survive in an artificial city? Perhaps referring to the strangeness of Brasília and its bizarre politics, a São Paulo newspaper cartoon (July 6, 2007) jokes that anyone in Brasília who is not already from outer space must have been abducted.

The Utopian city, once inaugurated, had to face reality, and its futuristic spaces and designs were suddenly filled with all the problems of Brazilian society, as the influx of population began to change the design and uses of the city. There was a confrontation between architectural order and civic chaos, between bureaucracy and democracy in the daily life that sprang up, seemingly irrationally, in the few public spaces and sidewalks. Nature had been reinvented in Brasília, so that everyday activities, such as visiting the supermarket, became noble architectural excursions. Because the wide horizons and open spaces reduced the sense and image of human occupation, the city filled with migrants whose identity now became uncertain, open, and multiple. There was neither past nor future, only imagination and change. In daily life, however, citizens were obliged to face the high levels of violence, poverty, and instability that are the realities of urban Brazil. They lived lives in transition, in search of new identities to match the futuristic environment: either they would find a way to survive the city, or it would consume them, obliging them to return to their place of origin.

João Almino holds the rank of ambassador in the Brazilian

diplomatic corps, Itamaraty, which is housed in one of the architectural gems of Brasília.[7] Almino was, like everyone else, a newcomer to the capital. His novels set in Brasília are the first narratives to portray new residents of the city, adjusting to a different life in a futuristic setting. The novel *As cinco estações do amor* (*The Five Seasons of Love*, 2001) is his third, after *Samba-enredo* (*Theme-Samba*, 1994) and *Idéias para onde passar o fim do mundo* (*Ideas for Where to Spend the End of the World*, 1987). The three novels, whose characters embody the experience of life in Brasília, have precedents in Brazilian urban literature. Almino's narrator Ana, who looks out over Brasília's Lake Paranoá, has been considered a companion to Machado de Assis' characters Brás Cubas, in *Posthumous Memoirs of Brás Cubas*, or Rubião in *Quincas Borba*, who contemplate the Bay of Botafogo from their city residences. The influence of Portuguese realist Eça de Queirós has been seen in his circle of intellectuals and writers who were alienated from the bourgeois society of their time.[8] In twentieth-century Brazil, Almino's novel finds a parallel in Oswald de Andrade's portrait of the modernist city of São Paulo in 1922, with its psychological portrait of the character Alma, who struggles in urban depths of passions and betrayals.[9] Almino's Ana also brings to mind Clarice Lispector's heroines, who are existentially alienated from their useless, bourgeois lives as housewives in mid-century Rio de Janeiro. In Almino's Brasília, coming of age from the 1960s to the next turn of the century, urban characters continue to interact with the capital's idiosyncrasies, fighting to avoid meaninglessness and artificiality in their new lives. The group of friends in the novel, whose lives scatter and change unpredictably, call themselves "The Useless Ones." Ana's narrative weaves together the personal stories of these characters, who feel rootless and alienated in the futuristic environment. *The Five Seasons of Love* is a novel about change, adaptation, and survival under unexpected and strange circumstances.

Brasília the city is ever present, underlying the stories of the characters in *The Five Seasons of Love*. They live by the forms, spaces, and circumstances of the city around them, in which Utopian design confronts the demands of a growing population and the dynamics of contemporary urban life imported into the awaiting buildings and avenues. Change, whether social, personal, or political, marks the lives of all the characters. Personal change dominates the narration by a young woman who came to Brasília from a small town in Minas Gerais. Throughout her narrative, Ana is sorting and throwing out papers from her former life, which remind her of her ex-husband Eduardo, as she searches for a self that has been lost in the dissolution of the marriage and in her solitary life as a retired university professor. By ridding herself of accumulated papers, she symbolically erases all memory of the past, which she plans to recreate on blank pages, which are Brasília. Only the present moment holds together the stories of all the other characters, especially the "Useless Ones," her educated friends who meet in a local restaurant and bar.

Brasília's empty newness abolishes historical and personal memory. Change is already present in Ana's psychology in an alter–ego, the bold, confident, and assertive Diana, who may suddenly appear at any time. When she is Ana, however, she discards her previous identity, tries to be like the new city she has adopted by starting over, and empties out her previous life of its commitments and emotions:

> For an instant I still recall the adventure that brought me to the Central Plateau, as if to fulfill a mission. It occurs to me that from the beginning the monumental structure of Brasília defined the limits of that adventure of mine. Brasília is the heavy streaks of rain on the window, the noisy cars passing, the loneliness of a big city, death, unrequited love, anguish...

The city propels Ana into the future and makes her believe that the only possible view of life is instantaneism: "the acceleration of time doesn't allow us any option," she comments. When she looks at the horizon she witnesses what Lispector saw as calculated space, a Magritte transparency in surface reality:

> Everything in Brasília can be seen at a glance. In the clear skies and generous light, one's eyes see not just the horizon in the distance but also the dividing line between the city and the country. Predictable layout, expected curves. Behind this wide-open light and the evidence of what is planned, a mystery nevertheless persists.

When she goes out, the cityscape signals to her, monumentalizing the anonymity and emptiness she feels inside:

> I take Monument Avenue. Ahead of me, the neon quadrilateral at the National Shopping Center is lit. The red in the ads appears to continue into the sky. Across the crimson horizon the clouds trace spiral figures in smoke. Right in the center, an enormous reddish-gray question mark. In the middle of the sky and my life. A passing foreboding, that comes to me as a distraction...
> It is the autumn of the flowering quaresmas; in the still-green trees and grass. The clouds may unload more rain at any moment. But soon the long dry winter should begin; dreaded by all, except me, because the dryness agrees with my temperament, just like these empty vistas, punctuated by figures that crisscross them like little lost ants...

By the end of its first decade of existence, Brasília is already suffocating from the poverty and pressure of the eighteen satellite cities surrounding it and from the military dictatorship running the country. The satellite cities of Taguatinga and Ceilândia reach more than double the population of the capital, while Gama, Sobradinho, Planaltina, Guará, and Samambaia each pass the 100,000 mark by the 1990s. Examples of decay, crime, and change fill the streets and Ana's narrative. All new arrivals are viewed with suspicion. Ana's apartment is assaulted by thieves, perhaps involved with her cook's son. Her friends in the club of "The Useless Ones" have nearly all left the city. When Helena left to join a revolutionary group in the interior, security agents searched for her in Ana's apartment. Joana married a Rio entrepreneur and became a society matron when the rest of the Useless were still dressing like hippies. Norberto, a former boyfriend, left for San Francisco and returned as a woman to share Ana's house; the change of sex surprised Ana, and was not without its humorous side as she watched "Berta" awkwardly learn feminine ways. New political, psychological, and sexual identities belong in Brasília.

Brasília's pure modernity is strong in material and spirit, however, in spite of the social problems imposed on it, and is capable of offering a resurrection, as Malraux perceived, through the lyricism of its forms. Its new residents can discover and partake of this redeeming quality. Ana must discover the inner strength emanating from the city by a questioning and analysis of herself and the world around her through her narrative; she holds forth with the social world of friends, domestic servants, household pets, while continuing to discard her past and search for a fundamental point of new beginnings:

My youth is lost. The Brasília of my dream of the future is dead. I recognize myself in the façades of

its prematurely old buildings, in its unstable and
decadent modernity... I have no desire to leave
Brasília, or even leave the house. I don't need to.
From here I see everything, feel everything,
though it may be from the inside of the bell jar
that I created to preserve my discretionary space.
It's quite true that there is no difference between
remaining locked up here or in Taimbé. I have this
view over the Paranoá Lake, but I prefer to see
nature on television. Perhaps I have gone crazy,
this is how I live. I don't need to move. I don't
want to see anyone. I lock myself in with my
memories... I want to capture the moment, to
start from zero. Without any baggage from the
past. Without history, without direction.

The empty depths of Brasília's vast spaces and horizon miniaturize
Ana into just another lost ant on the vast plateau; she sets fire to her
papers and attempts suicide, in the abstract anonymous emptiness
of form without content:

A terrible black vision of the world surrounds me.
I have been devoured by life. I am the most
miserable of creatures. A black slave. A destitute
and mistreated woman. A street urchin. Landless.
A dying Jane Doe in a charity hospital. An
unknown pauper's body left to a teaching hospital,
then dissected in an anatomy class.

The vigilance and caring of Ana's neighbor, Carlos, however, saves
her life and offers her hope in the security of a changed identity that
enables her to begin life again in the artificial city. Others are not so
fortunate, however: Helena never returns from the guerilla

insurgency at Araguaia, and Berta, formerly Norberto, who takes her identity cards, is murdered in a hate crime. For Ana, a few weeks back in her hometown, Taimbé, are enough to convince her that her life and the new city's are now inseparable, and her only imperative is to accept the moment and live again. She accepts that personal change and new beginnings are possible, although at great cost, even in a futuristic city:

> In the Pilot Plan, roots take flight and beat their wings like butterflies. Who can guarantee that I am not artificial like Brasília? Taimbé is here, in my meeting Carlos. Minas is on the terrace of this house where Carlos and I are small town lovers. Where we are matters more than where we are going, or whence we have come... I have to rid myself of this weight, to begin the new century.

Ana's narrative tribulations are the basis for re-education in the life she must lead on her own in the futuristic city. She must learn to overcome the weaknesses of Brasília's Utopian, ultramodern design and vast spaces: form without substance, function versus pure idea, grandeur against intimacy. She has struggled with the urgency to create a new authenticity out of an almost metaphysical artificiality, and her narrative recapitulates the challenge facing migrants to the world's new global cities, a bet on life and the power to renew ourselves:

> Building a city from nothing is a bet on life. I want to live on the frontier that advances across the immense emptiness. To rebuild myself out of the ashes.

The Five Seasons of Love is a narrative for Brasília, the city, and the coming of age of its new citizens. Almino's novel of change, suffering, sacrifice, and adaptation answers the question everyone asked about a city built without inhabitants: how can anyone live there? It carries the once futuristic city across the millennium after four decades and tells the epic, mythical story of a first generation who had to learn how to live in it, starting from the vast emptiness and the centuries-old appeal of the central plateau.

K. David Jackson
Yale University
New Haven, 2007

[1] *Lettres à Nelson Algren: un amour transatlantique*, 1947-1964, texte établi, traduit de l'anglais et annoté par Sylvie Le Bon de Beauvoir, Paris, Gallimard, 1997, 525.
[2] "Brasília," *Jornal de Brasília*, Jun. 20, 1970.
[3] "Depoimento," *Modulo* 9, Rio de Janeiro, Feb. 1958, 3-6
[4] "Corolário Brasileiro," *Forma* 7-8 Rio de Janeiro, Mar.-April 1931, 20-22.
[5] André Malraux, *Palavras no Brasil*, org. and trad. Edson Rosa da Silva, Rio de Janeiro, Funarte, 1998.
[6] João Almino, "O mito de Brasília e a literatura," *Estudos Avançados,* São Paulo 21.59 (2007).
[7] There is a tradition in Brazil of distinguished authors who are also diplomats, including novelist João Guimarães Rosa and poet João Cabral de Melo Neto.
[8] "Pesadelos brasileiros no cenário da capital da República," *O Estadão*, São Paulo (7-7-2001).
[9] See Walnice Nogueira Galvão, *Musas sob Assédio: literatura e indústria cultural no Brasil*, São Paulo, Senac, 2005, 83-84.

THE FIVE SEASONS OF LOVE

1

ADVENTURES OF SOLITUDE

Everything starts when I receive the letter from Norberto, a little over a year ago, during two days of crisis and revelation. I can't avoid what is going to happen. Some mistakes only become apparent with experience, when we can no longer correct them.

It is one of those hot afternoons in Brasília. I lower the car window, put the revolver in my purse and start the car. I wave to Carlos. He is retired from the Congressional Library and spends hours planting roses of the most unusual colors, even some imported cuttings from France and the U.S. Another one of his passions is orchids, some potted, but most grafted onto two trees in the garden. I don't know if he loves his wife Carmen, and if he doesn't, it's because of his good taste. He loves flowers, particularly those roses and orchids. His silver hair shines in the sun. I'm always struck by his jovial air, and above all by the serenity evident in his voice and his measured gestures. He loves soccer and sometimes goes out wearing the Flamengo jersey to play a pick-up game.

"Life is like soccer," he had said. "It's hard to score a goal, but the more we try the better our chances." He brightens with a smile when he sees me and asks me to wait. He admires me, nurtured by his notion of the quality of my library and by some silly thing or other that I wrote. He was one vow away from becoming a priest. He left the robes for Carmen. He knows Greek and Latin. He spent his

3

life surrounded by books but according to him he never kept any at home, and this is why, having left his job at the library, he wants to consult mine. Berenice, my housekeeper, committed the indiscretion of announcing my birthday to the world, and now I spot the fragile petals of a red rose picked for me, against Carlos' massive and muscular torso. Who wouldn't like to receive a rose? It enhances the colors of this afternoon when a yellow light bathes the landscape.

Diana would sashay over in her miniskirt to receive this rose. She would tell Carlos that she adores seeing him take care of his garden and this story would have another beginning. Diana is my flip side who has always lived inside me. I should have been registered as Ana, the name my parents had jointly agreed upon. But Diana was the first name Mother wanted to give me, a spontaneous choice that not by chance is also the one that appears on my birth certificate. Since Father was against it, they ended up calling me Ana, which is how I'm known. So sometimes I imagine myself Diana, doing what I fear, saying what I silence. She always has the answer on the tip of her tongue. I bite my tongue. This is how it works: when I am who I am, I'm Ana. When I am who I want to be, I'm Diana. She is me as pure desire. We are quite similar, identical twins. Diana extends me. She extends my spirit, my body – being even taller, she softens the fullness and curves I have acquired over time – and also my skin, since she has no wrinkles and not even a hint of cellulite. She is as dark-skinned as I am. I adore my dark complexion.

Because I am Ana, I contain myself. The most I dare is to wear this pink spaghetti strap dress, black hose, red shoes and handbag. I took two long baths, tried a new shampoo recommended by my hairdresser – he cut my hair too short, which I fear calls undue attention to my nose – and I lavished myself with Boticário body lotion.

If I haven't dated since my divorce from Eduardo, it's not because I haven't recovered from the scandal of our separation. It's that I learned certain things about men. I divide them into three categories: those that are better avoided, the harmless, and the ones worth provoking, just provoking. I prefer to refuse them all, although

I still fantasize about a great love, thinking that I'll find someone who will really be my companion. I feel particularly powerful, a power that I manipulate with my body, when refusing the overtures of important men. Actually, I have to admit, candidates don't appear or, when they do, they're married, in search of a little fling. I include Carlos – and his charming open smile, his gesture of bringing me a rose – potentially in this category, although for the first time I notice something different in his look, perhaps due to my dream.

A horrific dream. I was kidnapped by bandits who demanded cash. I didn't have the money and they wouldn't take my credit card, which was too thick, so thick that it wouldn't swipe through the machine. I had a piece of property inherited from Father that was going to be expropriated. I didn't even know how much it was worth, the government was going to appraise it, and it was finally Eduardo, my ex-husband, who was going to pay the ransom. One of the bandits, who looked like Pezão, my housekeeper Berenice's son, had tied my wrists. He was on top of me and forced my legs open. By some miracle I freed my hands, managed to grab the revolver in my purse and fired. Blood spewed from the boy's face, and then I noticed that he was a boy, an unarmed child crying for food. Hunger lived in that child, and had ever since he was born as I could see from his ribs. The boy was the same one I had seen on the television ads for a UN program in Africa, it must have been Biafra or Somalia, and I felt terribly guilty. I would be arrested for not giving him the food he asked for and what's more, for having committed a heinous crime. Well then: the corpulent police officer who arrested me with heavy handcuffs was my neighbor Carlos who looked at me with utter indifference as if he didn't know me.

It's easy to understand the presence of Pezão in this long and terrifying dream. Ever since he lost his job I've paid him a half salary to come once a week to take care of the garden. He's dark-skinned and handsome and has already caused me a lot of trouble; one day the police dragged him off to Papuda Prison, accused of auto theft. He was thrown into a filthy cell, crushed like a canned sardine, waiting for me to intercede. As a matter of fact, that day I had to seek the help of the friend who has invited me to dinner now, Chicão – it's to his apartment that I am headed – because I'm deathly afraid of the police, and not just because of the old paranoia from the days of the dictatorship; it's also because I know that the police are in collusion with criminals, with the drug dealers. I think Pezão smokes crack and even Berenice worries that he keeps bad company. I fear that he and my nephew Formiga – whom no one knows by his real name Rogério – belong to a gang.

It's also obvious why Eduardo appeared in the dream. My house still reminds me of him, and I've had financial difficulties. After my traumatic separation, I got the house, the furniture, and the artwork. No alimony. I had to live on my modest salary as a university professor. Of the gifts he gave me the only one that keeps me company is the gold lighter that helps me light one cigarette after another.

I take the Grand Axis. Ahead of me, the neon quadrilateral at the National Shopping Center is lit. The red in the ads appears to continue into the sky. Across the crimson horizon the clouds trace spiral figures in smoke. Right in the middle, an enormous reddish-gray question mark. In the middle of the sky and my life. A passing foreboding, that comes to me as a distraction.

Autumn is in the flowering *quaresmas*; in the still-green trees and grass. The clouds may unload more rain at any moment. But soon the long dry winter should begin; dreaded by all, except me, because the dryness agrees with my temperament, just like these empty vistas, punctuated by figures that crisscross them like little lost ants.

I called Chicão as soon as I received Norberto's letter. It never crossed my mind to celebrate my birthday. In fact, I had decided to do nothing, absolutely nothing; I was going to stay home. "How depressing!" Chicão protested and convinced me to accept his invitation to "our trivial little supper," as he defined it. It would be just us – me, him and his companion, Marcelo.

I live almost all alone and surrounded by few friends. Friendship develops more easily in the midst of the irresponsibility and scheming of youth. With age my quota of friends has declined, and today it is filled. I'm lucky to still have Berenice, my housekeeper, and my niece and nephew, Vera and Formiga, who have lived with me ever since the death of my sister Tereza. Her youngest, Juliana, seven and very cute, stayed in Taimbé with Regina, my other sister. Regina herself prefers that the older ones live with me; in Brasília they can get a better education.

I still have the company of my dog Rodolfo and my cats Lia and Leo, both with the same long white fur, and the same black around their yellow eyes. The three of them live together in perfect harmony. I bought Leo and Lia mainly to deal with the rat that lives in the kitchen and that seems to have a thorough knowledge of rattraps, because he always manages to avoid them. Sometimes when we come across him, he runs under the refrigerator and Berenice, Vera and I escape onto the chairs. Formiga has no fear of the rat and for this reason defends him; there's no reason to hunt the poor animal. Rodolfo on the other hand doesn't scare him. They've become best friends.

Rodolfo always comes to greet me at the door with his tail wagging for joy. I prize this gift from Norberto, these fifteen years later, more than all the nonsense he's written to me ever since he went to São Paulo and from there to Lisbon. He's a mutt with the soul, features, and even the beige color of a Lab. The name Rodolfo came to me for no reason. I thought of Rodolfo Valentino. Chicão thinks that I wanted to ridicule someone we knew, Rodolfo Vaz. But the animal just looked like a Rodolfo, a face with that name, be it Valentino or some other Rodolfo.

I associate friendship with the period of the Useless; that was what we called ourselves thirty years ago. It was Chicão's idea; he always preached passivity. "Action transpires more from ignorance than from knowledge," he used to say. Ever since then, I haven't made any true friends. Without realizing it, time became a rare commodity and did away with the accessibility that all friendship requires.

Of the Useless, besides me, only Chicão and Japona still live in Brasília. I see Japona very rarely, always by accident. I get news of him from his daughter Monica who's a friend of my niece and nephew. I was only in his house in the North Peninsula once. He owns a farm, a small market in the entrequadra and the restaurant Delícias de Minas, in 204 South. At the time of the Useless, it was already apparent that his pragmatic spirit would take him far. He was always saying that São Paulo was a success because of the Japanese blood. But Chicão says that he never saw him as Japanese or as an entrepreneurial capitalist, but rather as an Indian from the Plateau. That suspicious look, that straight black hair cut in bangs, Beatles style, must have been from some local tribe. Our gang preferred to call him Japona and not his nickname Tatá, which only remotely recalled his real surname, Tanabe.

Male friends, only Chicão, to whom I can open up without worry; with whom I argue and make up. He would never trick me; he'd always defend me. When our opinions differ, curiously enough our desires in some way mesh, tempered by steady gentle warmth. Opinion does not define friendship. What counts are the feelings for one another, the affection, the tenderness. It's knowing that when I complain Chicão listens to me and tries to understand. With him I can cry, as I cried when Father died, knowing that he would comfort me. Between us there are no demands, no ceremony or bootlicking. It's to his apartment in 308 North that I'm headed on this hot afternoon with the rose that Carlos gave me pinned to my dress, to celebrate my fifty-fifth birthday and to talk about serious and not-so-serious things; politics and other worldly misfortunes.

Besides Chicão I don't know whom else to include among my friends. I have always feared Joana's feelings toward me. Just thinking about her makes me uneasy. But she was totally loyal to me when the Eduardo scandal broke. And at the age of twenty-one it was with her that I stayed when I arrived in Brasília. I had met her two years earlier on vacation in Belo Horizonte.

From the sixth floor window of her apartment in 105 South we could see the lake that reflected the days' moods and the hills that climbed the horizon. As they say in Minas, from a distance every hill is blue. Above those hills dark heavy clouds foreshadowed sinister things, but my superstition did not interfere with grand dreams. Brasília was "the modern city and the future of the world," as Father always said. If he had money he would have bought property in Goiânia and South Lake. The Pilot Plan was not exactly a city. It was an idea – an idea of modernity, the future, my idea of Brazil.

For me it was like jumping over a wall and falling into the heart of the nation, a heart that beat like mine. With the butterfly shape given by Lúcio Costa, Brasília was a free point in an empty space, with the ability to fly and grow in any direction. Its ethos oscillated between the infinite heavens and the dark wet mud – where with pleasure I dirtied my feet, and that contrasted with the clean highways and the green spaces organized into large quadrangles.

A new city, a new life. Arriving at night, my eyes shone before the carpet spattered with rows of lights that spread like rays in all directions. Those flames of mystery and hope twinkled for me. Their astonishing beauty made my stomach churn. That's how I arrived in Brasília, with the illusion of adventure and freedom.

In the landscape I imagined a lifestyle, a Planalto way of being. Daring and elegant. Simple and direct. Coarse and modern. As if the confident natives of Brasília had sprouted from the hard life of the Northeasterners. There was a certain style in men or women from Brasília even if no one was born there. Perhaps it was that very foreignness, that not-belonging belonging. That shared awe before the immense sky, that excess of ground. The imagination sparked by the freedom and lightness of those concrete slabs, defying the engineers' numbers. The stubbornness in undoing the clean design, the straight lines and the soft curves of the architects. And this with the chaotic spontaneity stamped on the dirty walls and the sinuous paths. It's easy to understand why the Russian astronaut Yuri Gagarin thought that Brasília looked like another planet.

I met Joana's friends right away: Helena, Eva, Maria Antônia, Japona and Chicão. Joana always noticed everyone's tiny faults; that was her entertainment. She didn't even spare her friends. She complained about everything, from the mattress to the shoes, from the weather to the amount of salt in the food. But she accepted the dictatorship without any problem, claiming she had no interest in politics.

A month later, when I began to share an apartment with Helena and Maria Antônia, Joana told me that she only forgave Helena because she danced well and was the life of every party. But I should be careful with her friends. Even today, it's as if I can see Helena right here, her dark frightened face without makeup, her curly hair, arguing animatedly. Sometimes she argued that she would not accept that the army called their coup d'état a "revolution," sometimes she thought that one of us seemed to think like a reformist and not a true revolutionary. And sometimes she argued for so many other reasons arising from the ambiguity of living between the drug scene and political activism. Being five years older, she saw me as naïve and inexperienced.

My room was simple: white walls, a poster, a few books, a Northeastern hammock bought in Taguatinga, and already an enormous accumulation of objects and papers. It was a hardship for my parents, but until I could find a job I gratefully accepted their support. They sent me enough money for my basic expenses.

At a party in the apartment I shared with Helena and Maria Antônia, Chicão baptized the gang as "the Useless," and we agreed that we would meet every Thursday at the Beirute Bar. Confident of our inherent goodness and of our wisdom born from a rediscovery of our own inner nature, unguarded with each other, it was not success, power or money that we wanted. It was to change society, politics, the nation, the world. And we would succeed, or so we thought, because we were not alone; the future was ours. We were companions on a pleasure trip; we would build a new era, opposed to selfishness and squareness.

I had arranged my transfer to the University of Brasília. And my routine became: university, gatherings at the Beirute on Thursdays, and parties on Saturdays.

Joana didn't go to the Beirute, and when she broke with Helena because of "class struggle," she stopped coming to the parties. "If it's a matter of class struggle, we should defend our own," she would say. Helena called her a "Fascist" and they stopped speaking to each other.

Around that time Joana started seeing a much older man, an entrepreneur from Rio, that Rodolfo Vaz who Chicão says inspired my dog's name. Six months later, to our surprise, she married him and moved to Rio. Only Eva brought news of her every so often, and it was at a party she gave at her country house near Planaltina that Joana, passing through Brasília, met Cadu for the first time. That was why, although she had introduced me to almost all the Useless – even Cadu, at that same party – Joana was never part of the group that later became larger with the arrival of Norberto and the Philosopher.

Joana was also responsible for introducing me to Eduardo, the only time I visited her in Rio. She lived in a penthouse apartment on Vieira Souto. She had become a socialite. At a time when following Eva's example we made a point of dressing like hippies, she wore designer dresses, high-heeled shoes and heavy make-up. The apartment was decorated with an expensive beauty that I would call metallic, a studied vulgarity. The only personal touch was the collection of paintings that Joana said she had been acquiring over the years as an investment, most of which, according to her, was in storage for lack of space.

To show me a canvas that she praised constantly she took me to her room – along with Eduardo, whom she had introduced as a friend of Rodolfo Vaz. It was a portrait of herself, although the woman portrayed front face, with a frigid expression, was unrecognizable. Secretly she told me that her fingerprints were imprinted on it and that snips of her hair, and even her pubic hair, besides scraps of the clothes she had worn on her honeymoon – her dress, her hose, her bra, her panties – and a shoe heel were glued to it.

Later I wet myself laughing with Eduardo; I always liked a man who could make me laugh, it was laughter that connected us, joined our spirits, while a drizzle had started to fall... We were strolling down the beach sidewalk talking about Joana's cleavage, her pubic hairs stuck to the painting, Rodolfo Vaz's ridiculous sideburns contrasting with his baldness… I can picture, as if it were today, the noisy street like an endless hallway; the car headlights illuminating Eduardo's profile; the Arpoador rock strange in the dusk; his laugh as he sat across from me in the bar. It was passion at first sight. He had a very different sensibility from mine. That attracted me.

We had a long-distance relationship, he in São Paulo, I in Brasília. That passion consumed me to the point of distancing me from the Useless. I continued to share the apartment with Helena and Maria Antônia, until each went her own way. Maria Antônia moved to São Paulo. Helena left her documents with me. She didn't want to burn them, and to keep them could endanger her. When she left she told me: "Some day I'll send you word." I understood that she was going to take a new identity and make "the true revolution" as she liked to call it, contrasting the revolution that "would be" with the one the army had staged.

Cities acquire the air of the times through which they pass. Brasília, that once had been the promise of socialism and, for me personally, of freedom, no longer wore this mask. The desolation of the satellite-cities was already suffocating it. Twenty-four hours a day we breathed the poisoned air of the military dictatorship. Even in the classroom, we looked suspiciously on any newly arrived colleagues; one of them could be from the intelligence agency. That's why I agreed with Helena. The secret police were in fact looking for her. When they interrogated me about her whereabouts and searched my apartment, they accepted the truth as truth: in fact I didn't have the slightest idea where she had gone. On the other hand, in what could be one of the sources for my police panic, I began to have a nightmare that stayed with me for a long time, in which the police pursued me. I tried to scream, and my voice wouldn't come out; I tried to run and my legs skated in place.

Ever since then the Useless haven't seen each other. But the time for a reunion has arrived, as Norberto reminds me in the letter he wrote me from San Francisco – as evidence that those who disappear are in fact found there. And so, on this hot afternoon, I leave my house less to celebrate my birthday than to show Chicão the infamous letter that you need to read to believe. When I arrive, Jeremias, an inveterate bachelor and one of my former colleagues at the university, is also here. I keep in touch less and less with all of my extremely boring ex-colleagues. Later I demand of Chicão: "What's this? Trying to be a matchmaker?" A table of three would be very strange, he defends himself.

I usually disagree with Chicão, but I like, really like, his eccentricities. I enjoy hearing his monologues. A fulltime critic, he inveighs against any and all with his Gatling gun, without being genuinely interested in anything. An erudite Useless, as I've been saying. His prodigious memory leaves mine in the dust. He remembers everything: names, dates, entire film dialogs and even conversations that he hears. He won a television game in which he answered questions about Papal history. I don't care that deep down he's a conservative and that ever since I've known him he's been dead weight in his job with National Heritage.

On this night I want only one thing: for him to help me decide whether or not to answer Norberto's letter and most of all whether I should agree to let him stay with me. It has been more than thirty years since Norberto joined our group one night at the Beirute. He was likable and his guitar and his voice had charmed us, ranging across a repertoire that went from tangos to sambas, passing through *bossa nova* and arriving at *tropicalismo*. His features were as dark as the soil of the Plateau, angular as the outlines of the landscape and at the same time angelical, with his eyes like Alain Delon's in *Rocco and His Brothers*.

The Philosopher once said that each face reveals its trajectory and projects it into the future. In Norberto's I saw poverty, the suffering and sadness of his childhood, and foresaw the refined free native son of Brasília, determined to extract milk from a stone if necessary, to discover meaning in the emptiness of the Central Plateau. If there was a Brasília man, for me he was it. He gave me his telephone number, and I spent a week thinking how I was going to gather the courage to call him.

Even then, Diana and Ana coexisted inside of me. Diana, the adventurer; Ana, the cautious. Diana, the brave; Ana, who suffered the havoc of courage. I took up my Diana self:

– I want to see you because I can't forget your face.

– So I'm only a face to you?

– I had to call you, before it was too late.

– Too late for what?

Perhaps I meant to say "too late for love," but I didn't reply.

We arranged to meet. It would be better if we met just for coffee. Although I had called him so that I didn't feel like a coward, I didn't want to rush things. I was all Ana and immediately regretted having called, I was only looking for trouble. But he was so charming… The most handsome man on earth. I was attracted by his dark complexion, high cheekbones, square chin, imperfect nose and cat eyes; all wrapped up in a delicate and innocent air.

We went to the Swiss Patisserie, at the beginning of the South Wing. Born in the countryside to a poor family, he had arrived when he was twelve with the laborers during the construction phase. He had seen Brasília when it was nothing, a houseless field. He had made his life alone. His passion was drawing – he drew mostly faces, with ease, using pencil or pen and ink. If he could he would have made a living at it.

I attributed his evasive behavior to a supposed shyness, which only served to increase my attraction to him. When he agreed to see me again he asked me if I didn't have a boyfriend. I blurted out: "I don't know what the future of our relationship will be." And for many days the echo of his silence tortured me.

We went out other times and confirmed that we had much in common. With time, my affection for Norberto reached a point where he was never out of my thoughts; he occupied all of my daydreams. Finally Diana became impatient. With no regard for the consequences she spoke openly about what she felt, that his looks had perturbed her from the first time she saw him; she was in love with him.

I shouldn't take it the wrong way, he responded; he liked me, and that's why he had to show his cards. Crying, he confessed his predilections. He spoke of his friend, Cláudio Reis, who came to be the Philosopher of our Useless group. I should believe that he loved me, truly loved me, but it was a love without sex. I was not interested in sex with him, I responded, I just wanted him to hold me, and we embraced, enveloped in tender feelings that moved us both to tears.

"I want you to be my friend, my friend for always," he proposed. And I responded sincerely to his outpouring, I also wanted to be his friend always. Whatever I came to be, whether I became rich or poor, whether I married or not, he would continue to matter to me, I would always be interested in him; two old people, we would be side by side sharing our desire to change the world, exchanging ideas, admiring beautiful things, laughing at the ridiculous. "I want to do your portrait, a portrait to seal our friendship," he said. An oil painting, his first and perhaps only one.

I posed for hours on end, day after day. I think that because of his lack of experience with painting he made mistakes, mainly in accentuating the features of my face that began to look wrinkled and somber. I convinced Norberto not only to keep the painting, which he wanted to destroy, but also to deepen that tendency at which the painting hinted. Nothing to do with Dorian Gray. He should not paint me young. Better to portray me old, preferably as if I were at the end of my life, so that I could look at myself in the mirror of death, without fear of the passage of time, vaccinated against wrinkles and suffering. So that our friendship, which would last forever, would be sealed by the image of my end. "I want to anticipate all life's misfortunes, particularly old age, so that the future no longer frightens me," I explained.

We pricked our fingers with a tiny needle. With a little of our blood, plus red ink, Norberto added some light brushstrokes onto the canvas, on one side of my elderly face. And with the same mixture he signed it below, in the right-hand corner.

Weeks later, when we spent a weekend in the country house of a couple who were friends of Eva near Pirenópolis, we had already accepted as normal that Norberto and the Philosopher would hug and kiss in front of everyone. We all had in common that we could not be old fogies. Squareness was to be a virgin, stuck up, too prissy, in favor of the military, not drink, not smoke pot...

That weekend, I mentioned to Helena my frustrated attempt at dating. "Oh, don't tell me that you didn't even suspect!" Norberto frequently cross-dressed, put on lipstick, rouge, and a redheaded wig and made the scene at the descent to the Main Axis, near the National Hotel, she told me. She was known as Shirley and had a preference for shaven-headed recruits. I was furious. Shit! Why hadn't she told me before?

Thinking it over, the reunion that Norberto now calls for in the letter I show to Chicão arises from Eva's suggestion on that weekend. She was the muse of our group, admired and listened to. She wasn't pretty, she had a rather chubby body, but she was stylish – or better, anti-stylish. If she could have, she would have been at Woodstock. She had tried acid, was a vegetarian and called herself anti-capitalist. I was attracted by her lifestyle. As much as I tried, I never managed to copy her.

For the first time our group was complete, with the presence of Cadu, invited by Eva. I thought he was gorgeous: tall, thin reddish beard, light hair... High on drugs, he carried a Super 8 over one shoulder and a camera over the other. He suggested we take off our clothes and go skinny-dipping in the river. Prudish to be shocked by this proposal. I claimed the water was cold. Eva easily removed her Indian clothes to get in. Only she and her host friends accepted Cadu's invitation. There was no naturalness in his gestures. Or perhaps that was his true masculine naturalness. He didn't hide his fascination. He particularly didn't take his eyes off the bathers' genitals, and one could see his, slightly excited, swaying to the movement of his body.

Eva's friends, the couple who owned the country house, were knowledgeable about trees and animals. We took an oxcart ride along the edge of the river and heard lessons about snakes. For the first time I was introduced to a candeal tree. I sipped the resin collected directly from the stem of the jatobá, where drops fell into a little cup. Eva's friend explained that it was good "for weakness, cough and bronchitis." We heard about *guarás*, *guaxinins* and *moché*, a local name for toads. For dinner, rice with *pequi* fruit and a salad of *guariroba*, a kind of hearts of palm cut from trees on their own property. Later, we were outside, drinking sapoti liqueur and looking at the infinity of stars in a new moon sky.

Mysticism goes well with an environment like this one. In Brasília's urban landscape, Eva would not have been convincing as she told about her trips to the Garden of Salvation and talked about the prophetess Íris Quelemém, of whom we had heard. Besides Eva, none of us took the Garden of Salvation seriously, but we arranged to go there together. At least we were anthropologically curious, or perhaps Eva was right when she said that our materialism could not resist the slightest mystical call.

Our pact to meet again in 2000 – which Norberto reminds me of in his letter – arose about a month later when we took the mystical voyage to the Garden of Salvation, from which I brought this little jar of soil. Norberto didn't forget our agreement, made under lightning and a cold rain. In the letter, besides proposing to come live with me for a while so that we can plan the reunion, he reveals some news of his own that I intend to share with Chicão. He wants my blessing and sends a photograph so that I "don't faint" when I see him. He hopes that I approve of his new look and asks me not to tell anyone... His voice has changed, he's nothing like Norberto, Norberto is the past. He's even changed his name. He has been calling himself Berta, but now it will be different; he had surgery to become a woman. That's why he wants to officially change his papers and plans, with my help, to take over Helena's identity, since he remembers that folder with her documents... The photograph that accompanies Norberto's letter is of a woman in her early fifties, with puffy blonde lacquered Barbie hair. I almost don't recognize him. The delicateness of the features is accentuated – the chin bones are more rounded, the nose more perfect – but it contrasts with the thick masculine neck.

– I'm full of doubts. To begin with, the Useless no longer mean anything to each other. I never would have proposed this reunion – I explain to Chicão, after unwrapping the glass lamp that he and Marcelo gave me, and the CD, a gift from Jeremias.

Chicão taps the tobacco in his pipe, lights it and begins to throw his puffs into the air. His sixty years aren't noticeable, particularly since he no longer has white hair and his beard, now equally black, is better kept than ever.

– Ana, I insist you speak at the conference I'm organizing. Maria Antônia agreed to come. With Chicão present, there will be three Useless together – Jeremias interrupts.

Marcelo runs down the articles of the Penal Code infringed by Norberto if he uses Helena's identity. Just like a lawyer.

– She could even still be alive – he says.

– Just because they never found her body? That doesn't prove anything. Some are still missing. It's more than likely she was murdered – I point out.

– Some day she'll revive – Marcelo rebuts.

Enveloped in the smoke from his pipe, Chicão has no comment.

– Let's trade Helena for a whiskey – he proposes.

I have three and, like him, I don't stop smoking.

– But is it worth calling the reunion? – I ask. I don't even have all of the addresses; Cadu's, for example…

You just have to call Joana – Chicão says.

– Precisely what I don't want, because then I would have to invite her too. After all, she was never part of the group.

– Do you think that gigolo still has the nerve to be supported by Joana? – Marcelo needles.

– He's still alive, is he? I thought he had died – Jeremias, who barely knows Cadu, maliciously insinuates.

I don't like to hear that, because a few years ago he almost did die of an overdose. Chicão turns to me:

– Don't tell me that even you find that imbecile charming?

– I wonder if he's still a pervert in his old age – Marcelo continues.

– A pervert, with no luck – Chicão clarifies.

I regret having recalled the poor fellow's name.

– Eva committed suicide because she couldn't stand being married to him – Marcelo asserts.

– Just because of his affair with Joana? Eva never even suspected. She killed herself from too much vitality. She wasn't up to her own illusions – Chicão philosophizes.

I return to the topic that interests me:

– Don't you think that the situation is too crazy? Organize a reunion, ok. I also have nothing against Norberto having an operation. It's his body, his life... Now, wanting to come early, spend I don't know how many months with me and, worse, adopt Helena's identity. Yes, that bothers me.

– All you need to say is that you have no intention of organizing any such reunion. Presto, the reason for him to come disappears – Jeremias once again sticks his nose in where he wasn't invited, but this time I'm grateful for the sound advice.

– That's the best option – I agree.

We all go into the kitchen.

– If I had known you were without a maid, I wouldn't have accepted the invitation – I say.

– Nonsense. I love to cook. The ground beef stew is done, and Marquinhos is already asleep – Chicão reassures me. Marquinhos, three, is their adopted son.

– Our slave was too uppity, very demanding. Just think; she wanted three times the minimum wage. We couldn't afford to keep her. Look, you're lucky to have loyal, dedicated Berenice – Marcelo says to me.

At the table, as if he were going back on his own advice, Jeremias informs me:

– I have Maria Antônia's address.

– So do I. When I go to São Paulo I still see her – I explain.

– Now it's her tits that are in the air, not her ass – Chicão declares, in the grave and sonorous tone that does justice to his voluminous bearing.

– Chicão, behave yourself! – Marcelo orders. He has a habit of controlling Chicão and of disciplining him like a good lawyer: "Don't blow smoke in Ana's face, Chicão! Don't say this, Chicão! Don't say that!"

– Cadu was fixated on her derrière – Chicão continues.

Deep down I tend to agree with Chicão regarding those upright tits, if I indeed understand what he means. In fact, over time Maria Antônia put some distance between us. She's never going to come down off her pedestal to soothe a disgraced ex-friend.

Jeremias, fascinated that we know Maria Antônia so intimately, showers us with questions about her. Later, in what seems to be a veiled criticism, he simply states:

– Maria Antônia is involved with the landless movement. For her, agrarian reform can only happen by force.

After dinner, Chicão shows me a posthumous edition of the Philosopher's thesis on Husserl that has just been published. He died five years ago of AIDS. At the time Maria Antônia called from São Paulo to tell me. I didn't go. I didn't know the family… I sent a telegram.

He was thin and red-haired. He spoke softly, always with a smile on his lips. He caused an enormous sensation when he appeared at the Beirute the first time, taken by Norberto. "Pleased to meet you. I'm Cláudio Reis," he stammered, timid and formal. He showed us a little book of poetry that he had published himself and distributed in bars. That was the only time that we all had a serious discussion. "Marxism is a kind of Platonism," he pontificated. Being an outsider and a student of philosophy contributed to his assertion falling into the good graces of Chicão and the claws of Maria Antônia. "This is our Philosopher," Chicão declared, giving him the nickname that he never lost.

While I flip through the Philosopher's book and the conversation continues in monologues by Chicão, Marcelo starts to nod. It's his habit. After a certain hour, there's no way. He ends up sleeping on the sofa. Jeremias then says goodnight.

– Perhaps there is a definitive reason not to receive Norberto.

Regina is insisting that I go back to Taimbé, which is making me lose sleep. She says that Mother has been praying for the salvation of my soul... and she still wants me to return! Mother really does miss me. But it's probably because she needs someone to take care of her and because, despite all the time and distance, she thinks she can still control me – I comment to Chicão.

– Imagine the worst: that you accept your sister's invitation. Any Taimbé must be better than Brasília – he surmises.

– It's quieter, that's for sure. Which is not hard, let's agree on that. I never imagined that I could reach the point of buying a gun. Formiga, my nephew, convinced me of the need. Used, two hundred reais. Thirty-eight caliber, the so-called big three eight. I got a permit without having fired a shot. By now I've tested it a number of times, practicing at a firing range, and I can stand its recoil quite well. It handles easily.

– But don't you have that wild beast, Valentino, over there? – Chicão always called Rodolfo, Valentino.

– Oh, him, there's nothing brave about him. He was always lazy; he wags his tail for any stranger. Anyway, even if he were a wild beast, little good it would do.

– Then let's decorate him with our medal of honor of uselessness! Now, seriously Ana: you should get rid of that revolver.

– I don't expect to use it. I'm sure that it will stay on top of my wardrobe, collecting dust, for years at a time.

– You didn't buy a gun, you bought a tranquilizer...

Except that, deep down, the revolver makes me in fact extremely un-tranquil, I notice. Who hasn't heard of a person who killed himself in his own home just because he had a gun? Things like the boy who found the revolver in a drawer and killed his sister while playing? Or the father who heard a burglar prowling and only discovered that it was his son after killing him? I keep the revolver on top of the wardrobe, but there's always the risk of some unsuspecting person knocking it off, causing it to fire accidentally. I have to keep it loaded, otherwise it would be useless in an emergency, I observe.

After Marcelo retires, I take the opportunity to confide to Chicão what Diana drags out of me with great difficulty:

– I'm becoming depressed.

I don't reveal many other things I'm thinking: that my menopause was unrelenting; it was useless to take calcium and vitamin complexes; that everything has fallen, breasts, ass and mainly the desire and will to live; that I have become more impatient…

– And your classes? Your students? – Chicão asks me, constantly releasing puffs from his pipe.

– Didn't you know I had retired? I don't need to do a thing. For the first time I'm a free woman – I announce in a playful tone.

– Enjoy yourself then. Women were the ones who invented work, but really they were made for adventure and pleasure. Men are the ones who live for these daily obligations.

– What a chauvinistic idea!

– But, look – he changes his tone of voice, as if he were stating something serious – if you want to take on a noble task, you are precisely the one who should organize the reunion – he suggests, without mentioning my drama, bringing, as usual, an ironic smile to the wrinkles around his mouth. – I just finished reading an article about the millennia throughout history that says that neither the catastrophic nor the optimistic predictions have come to pass. You should contribute so that at least one prediction comes true: that the Useless will meet.

– We didn't make a prediction, but rather a promise.

I don't blame Chicão for my decision: from this moment I'm sure that it will be better to receive Norberto. The preparation for the reunion of the Useless will be, in fact, a noble task for me.

I'm scared to death to drive alone at this hour. I don't ask Chicão to come with me only because it would be absurd. I look around me. The block is dead. Only the gatekeeper in his booth. I stamp out my last cigarette on the sidewalk and, with my heart beating, I think how it might be better to stop carrying the revolver in my purse.

I turn on the car radio, "Cláudio Santoro," a female voice announces. I am inebriated by the violins and by the lights on the poles pouring over my eyes through the car windshield. Although I continue to wear my wristwatch so that I don't lose all sense of time, it has little to do with my internal clock. It only serves to punctuate my repetitive movements, my daily monotony.

When I get home, I give an especially big hug to Rodolfo, who as always comes to greet me at the door. He's here recording the passage of the years and of my friendship with Norberto. He has become patient and sleepy. He's nothing like that restless demanding dog of the old days. As a pup, he chewed on the carpets and carried my shoes around the house. It was hard for him to learn to do his business only outside. Sometimes he ran loose on the street and he soon became known to all the neighbors. He was too intelligent to obey me.

I find a vase of red and white roses, accompanied by a card from Carmen and Carlos – in his handwriting – with congratulations on my birthday. How sweet!

Berenice is asleep. Vera's light is on. She studies theater; she's studious but a flirt. Sometimes she stays on the phone until all hours. Formiga hasn't returned. He's a headache; he has no interest in studying. He smokes pot. He wants to make videos, but he just gets into trouble, hangs out with his group of friends, including Pezão, and gets home in the wee hours, especially since he bought a used car with my help.

I suspect that I am failing in my job to raise them. It's a generational problem; my parents instilled moral values, honor, dignity, and above all duty. We had to act with principles, courtesy, goodness, and compassion. We thought that effort and suffering made us better and more complete people. I grew up with a religious education, with precepts that later I stopped believing. It's true that I rebelled, but I never abandoned the values of honesty, sincerity, charity, and character integrity. I've always known the difference between right and wrong.

Sometimes I invoke my father's spirit, but without his religiousness, and being a skeptic and a pessimist, what can I teach my niece and nephew? I can't even be heard if my message is not one of freedom and pleasure.

I'm anxious when Vera or Formiga go out at night. Images of violent crimes appear before me, of them dying before I do. I recall the crimes that have marked this city's history, from the never–solved kidnapping and brutal murder of the girl Ana Lídia many years ago, to the more recent immolation of an Indian by boys who were out for a lark. I don't know my niece and nephew's friends, except for Mônica and Pezão. But I know they're part of a generation with no direction and alienated from the problems around them. Formiga spends the night out with friends; I don't know where they go. He denies taking heavy drugs… I fear that he'll go from pot to crack. Sometimes he comes home drunk, he says it was just a few beers… That's already enough to risk having a car accident. I also worry about Vera. I hear stories of girls her age who become mothers without considering the consequences. So I try to introduce the subject of the things she should do to be careful, because of AIDS. She disarms me, stating: "Believe it or not, Aunt Ana, I'm a virgin. And I am going to stay a virgin until I marry. It's my choice. Because without romanticism there's no point."

– A walk, Rodolfo? – I call. Lying at my feet, he lifts his head and wags his tail. I open the door for him to go out into the garden. I don't dare venture any farther; it would be risky to step outside.

These noises are not my imagination. I call Rodolfo inside. Someone is prowling around the house, I have no doubt. I get the revolver from my purse. I consider waking Berenice. From the window I see my neighbor Carlos, always at home, on guard duty. He's on the balcony, framed by the blue and white fake colonial of these Brasília houses, the newspaper open on his legs, a light illuminating the façade of the house and his pleasant face. His presence calms me. It occurs to me: we would stay up half the night, two retirees, keeping watch over the neighborhood, with his wife Carmen watching us. She's like Mother. She's nostalgic for a time that was never as rosy as she imagines, she laments anything modern and would like us to use horse and buggy and not have television or computers. Rodolfo opens his mouth in an enormous yawn, confirming that there's no reason for me to be concerned.

I go to Vera's room. She's in bed, listening to the radio and flipping through a magazine. On the walls, a mixture of icons: Che Guevara, Marilyn Monroe by Andy Warhol, James Dean, Madonna, Frida Kahlo, The Beatles, Caetano Veloso, and other younger ones that I don't know...

– What's this, Aunt Ana? – she cries, panicked at seeing the revolver.

– Don't you hear that noise?

She doesn't hear anything; she follows me to the living room, still startled; I regret having bothered her. And now I can't hear any noise either. I look through the gaps in the window: Carlos is no longer on the terrace.

Berenice awakens and I talk to her and Vera until Formiga arrives and sends me to bed. There's no burglar, it's just my imagination, he says, I hear too much, Rodolfo appears tranquil.

– Look, Rodolfo doesn't prove anything. He wouldn't get up even if I stepped on his neck. Didn't you see that he didn't even flinch when you arrived?

– But if it were a stranger, he'd warn us – Formiga replied.

Rodolfo reacts with one yawn after another.

It's all in my head, stimulated by the desire for something out of the ordinary to happen and that it, whatever it is, change me dramatically. But what out of the ordinary? Something to break the glass house that I have created where nothing ever happens? Where only a few people enter, all of them fictional, who have survived from my other lives? I want to go to the heart of the matter, the bottom of the well, without examining either the matter or the well. I want the moment of truth. But what truth?

Thus begins my fixation. I'm in a hurry for this unknown thing, as long as it's not my return to Minas. If it's not a burglary, then let it be a declaration of love, from someone with whom I can stroll

along the lake, telling him of my fear and the noises before dawn...
Someone who will make me forget an undesirable memory that is
always present: my mistake in having married, and worse, having left
Eduardo.

In essence, I await a new passion – blind, surprising and radical
like every passion – to knock me over. I await the revolution. As I
turn out the light in the living room I see in the dark my elderly face
painted by Norberto. I look at the features of the old woman in
whom I tried to see myself to prepare for the bald bearded time that
flies on quick wings, sidestepping misfortune, avoiding its traps, and
thus, manage to hang onto my youth.

My youth is lost. The Brasília of my dream of the future is dead.
I recognize myself in the façades of its prematurely old buildings, in
its unstable and decadent modernity.

I organize my creams on the dressing table. I undress before my
long vertical mirror, attached to the door of my wardrobe. I see
myself full-length – from the side, the back. With age, there's no way
to avoid this little belly. With exercise I manage to control the
cellulite. I refuse to have liposuction. I look at my wrinkles. How
much would a facelift cost? I apply face cream and reread Norberto's
letter carefully: "I'm insecure. After everything I've just told you, will
you still receive me? My character and my friendship are the same,
that I promise you."

I lie down thinking that the noises are real. If burglars break
into my house, they will actually do me the favor of rescuing me
from this monotony of waiting for heaven knows what, in which
anything good or bad remains in the realm of the potential. At least
something, as small as it might be, will happen, something that is
not just waiting for a revelation or returning in time, like returning
to Taimbé. Go back, no, never.

In my insomnia laced with noises and fear, I notice a cobweb
forming on the ceiling that mixes with the image of clouds that rose
this afternoon, interrogating me in the middle of the sky, in the
middle of my life. Even if nothing happens, I'm going to have an
internal revolution, the greatest of my life. I want to turn myself

inside out, my true self. I'm going to leave behind behaviors, traditions and ways of thinking, like old clothes that I should discard. This is a grandiose idea, because all of human history is inside me; it's a drama that moves my spirit.

I sleep poorly. I feel a horrible migraine and, when my sporadic menstruation starts in the early hours, I soak the bed with blood. I awaken with a heavy head. Then I get a sharp stomach pain. I think it's an ulcer, or worse, cancer. My legs are weak and a fever makes me shiver. It's the beginning of the end. On the living room wall, the painting that Norberto did reminds me of the inevitable that I still want to postpone. Contrary to all my expectations, perhaps I am that face already, or a more decrepit one.

I went through a gradual process of self-confinement. Surrounded by papers I closed myself in my own world. I read books by people whose company would never give me pleasure. Little by little, I find entertainment and company exclusively in books and no longer in people. In my imagination I become friends with authors, talk to them, so that I won't have to be annoyed by my former colleagues from the university. They're my virtual friends. They don't listen to me, they don't touch me, they don't praise me, they don't laugh at what I say, but I couldn't find more intelligent people in internet chat rooms. I also think about writing for those not yet born, the curious from the future. I talk with those who don't have today's prejudices and some day will understand me.

I have no desire to leave my bedroom. I don't even raise the shade. The light bothers me. The perfume of Carlos' roses on my night table is nauseating. The thermometer reveals a higher fever.

– Your condition is not serious, but if you like I can call the doctor – Berenice offers.

At times like this she takes good care of me. How many times hasn't she brought me breakfast in bed, Rodolfo following her around. Whenever anyone carries a tray, Rodolfo follows, hoping for some crumb as reward, even if the tray only has a glass of orange juice, a slice of papaya and a cup of coffee, like now.

– I won't leave Brasília, no matter how much Regina insists – I say.

— I'm homesick for Ceará.

— You tried to go back and couldn't adjust.

— Oh, I wouldn't go back to Ipiranga anymore, no. No one cares about me there. But I would live in Fortaleza.

I wish I didn't have a maid... Only Berenice is much more than a maid. She's my companion in misfortune. To say that she's my friend rings false, it sounds like demagoguery, cheap populism. And, as a matter of fact, with her I don't have a relationship of equals, as it should be between friends. She is sensible and clever, but her ignorance gets in the way of our communication. I only talk to her about the most trivial banalities. I let her take care of me. I need her company and depend on her for my mental health. I like her to be interested in me, in my minor daily doubts. There's no way to deny it, perhaps the word that defines what I feel for her is still "friendship," there's no better word, a simple friendship, born of familiarity and grown over time. I wouldn't ask her opinion about anything. Not even what dress I should wear. But she cares about me, likes me, wants to see me happy. I like her too, I want to see her happy.

"No one can be happy without friends," she once told me.

Berenice is closer to me than Maria Antônia, than Joana, obviously. Or Regina. Or even my niece and nephew. Or Mother, with whom I always had infernal fights. And Chicão is a man – even if not too manly. It's not possible to talk to him about certain things.

Looking out the picture window in the living room, while I smoke my cigarettes, I think about the time when I invariably used to lie by the pool on sunny days, and of how I have changed...

— Go back, I will never go back to Minas – I repeat out loud.

The weather is good. I bring the roses that Carmen and Carlos gave me to the balcony and take in some fresh air, with Rodolfo at my feet, enjoying the company of my niece and nephew Vera and Formiga.

— Aunt Ana, why don't you spend some time with Aunt Regina? – Formiga suggests. – Vera and I, we'll manage, take care of the house.

– Sure. Stay there a while, evaluate the situation – Vera says.

Those schemers. Since they don't see any good in this sick ornery aunt, they prefer to be left alone. I become irritated. They have to be patient and leave me alone, not moving, or wanting anything, looking at the roses that Carmen and Carlos gave me, that I didn't take care of as I should and that have started to wilt already. It does no good now to bring them onto the balcony and give them a dose of aspirin.

With Rodolfo always at my feet, I smoke non-stop, while ruminating on what's happening to me. The idea of my return to Taimbé grew after Father died, a death announced months before a late-diagnosed prostate cancer consumed him. Although he was quite old, it was a shock to me. He didn't have Mother's strong temperament; he was always gentle and understanding. He even understood my lack of interest in concrete things. He never demanded anything of me. He thought my failings were normal. He accepted my daring to leave home to study. For that alone I am eternally grateful. However, he was mistaken in the prediction that my future would be too large for the smallness of Taimbé. "Just don't forget about us, or your town," I still hear his voice. "Of course not," I answered, my eyes filling with tears.

Living in Taimbé would be a way to pay homage to him and to die in peace. I would go back there if Mother were not aging so poorly. She wants the best for me but she sees me as a child. I don't like either her intransigence or her harangues. She and Regina wouldn't be able to stand me for long either. I have no desire to leave Brasília, or even leave the house. I don't need to. From here I see everything, feel everything, though it may be from inside the bell jar that I created to preserve my intimate space. It's quite true that there's no difference between staying locked up here or in Taimbé. I have this view over the Paranoá Lake, but I prefer to see nature on television. Perhaps I have gone crazy, this is how I live. I don't need to move. I don't want to see anyone. I lock myself in with my memories.

– I think I'm going to die – I say.

— You're a hypochondriac, Aunt Ana. This is nothing more than the flu — Vera tries to convince me.

Returning to my room, already with the perspective of a dead woman, I ask myself what's the use of this pile of newspapers.

— Berenice, you don't need to buy the paper anymore!

Newspapers serve the daily function of inventing a form for the world. One believes in this form in order to enjoy the sensation of knowing where one is, but I have stopped trying to situate myself in the world.

— Buy a lottery ticket, instead of the paper.

Berenice thinks that's funny. Because it's the first time I've played, I have a feeling that I'm going to win big. I dream of this, I make plans. If I win the lottery, I'll change my life completely, without needing any other kind of revolution.

— Berenice, I've decided that I'll invite Norberto.

— You need to know first who he really is, right Miss Ana? You don't even know him anymore! A man who became a woman!?

— He says that his character hasn't changed; he's still my friend. And I'm not going to abandon a friend just because he had an operation. He was Eva's friend, too. — Berenice had great admiration for Eva, one of her first employers. She never failed to take flowers to her tomb on All Soul's Day.

— If you really want to…

— And if I advertise the room for rent?

— You'll never adjust to strangers living here, Miss Ana.

— The fact is I need money. But you'll see, I'll win the lottery. Or, you'll find a very rich boyfriend who'll feel sorry for this poor old woman and set us both up in a palace.

— Old nothing! You're a young thing and very pretty. — How good it is to have someone close by to repeat that once in a while!

Before I can rent the room or give it to Norberto, I need to empty it. My house is a landfill. In two bedrooms and the living room, there's no space for anything else. Berenice follows my orders to throw nothing away. And the kids are used to the objects, books and papers strewn around every room.

That's when I get the idea to write the story. My version of the life appraisal promised for the reunion. But nothing forced. I'll tell it with no deadline or objective. If I die, I'll leave the unfinished text with Chicão or Norberto himself.

I want to start with something out of the ordinary. But what extraordinary thing has ever happened to me? I'm simply a retired woman who, what's more, retired too early, because of the generosity of one law, and now is poorer because of the severity of another. I had an average life. Truly average. Nothing thrilling, picturesque, amusing, or heroic. Nothing exciting. No successful love story. No fantastic disaster. No tragedy capable of pulling heartstrings. Except for the scandal of Paulinho's story. But I won't write about that. My separation from Eduardo, even with bright colors, wouldn't be a plot for even the worst TV soap opera. My worst failing is being average. I live my life like a permanent daily tragedy, without a single detail that defines that tragedy. I even finished analysis – twice. Adventure is missing; a larger meaning for my existence, what one could call greatness. The sea is missing, and it's not because I live in Brasília. This is my tragedy. A tragedy that aches, not like chest pains. Like a predictable annoying migraine that I disguise as well as possible. I manage to disguise it quite well, and not just with my skin creams! With my Mona Lisa smile as well, where Jeremias thought he saw happiness. Or else I disguise it with hearty laughs, like the ones Chicão provokes in me. They cheer up my liver. They make me forget my melancholy. I feel better just visualizing him in his usual position, hooking his thumbs in his suspenders and pulling them forward, releasing his laughter along with an effusive rock of the chair.

Here I am looking at the blank pages on the desk. They expect an enormity of me: uncontained words, like red brushstrokes. Like blood. Like the blood on the painting that Norberto did of me, hanging on the living room wall. I still feel a fever, chills. May the emotion emerge from the ink in my pen, limpid and pure.

In my imagination I arrange the paints and select the brushes. I light one cigarette after another, which only worsens my condition.

I observe the smoke that rises from the ashtray, awaiting the lightning stroke of inspiration that is going to fall from the sky. Very soon I'll depart and, thus, this text will be the last thing I write. I will remain here writing until I die. Let Chicão and Norberto then show my story at the meeting of the Useless!

I grab a pen as if it were the revolver I bought. I point it at the paper, prepared to fire. Will it be possible to discover a meaning for disconnected facts? To find the right sentence that supports essential words, like life and love? I dissolve a large tube of red ink all over my memories, with the intention of leaving broad suggestive brushstrokes on the blank sheet. But nothing! On the paper only a white silence, a nerve-racking silence. Only a huge longing for I don't know what. Or... writer's block. I tear up the paper, furious.

I don't know if it's because of this block, for having thought about the promise by the Useless, for feeling ill or perhaps simply because the end of the millennium approaches, that I make the decision to clean out my papers, as if I were preparing to cross the tenuous line separating life from death.

I reread the letters from Maria Antônia at the time of Paulinho's disappearance, with her suggestion that I write my version of the events with all the details. Maybe she was right. Perhaps it was my responsibility. But the only biographical fact about me that would interest a wider public was my affair with him. And about that, what could I say? That Paulinho and I met when we were still children? That I saw him then as my future husband? That he was the part of me that was missing? That I loved him because I didn't have him? That I knew nothing, absolutely nothing, about his disappearance? That I believed the version that he had been killed by common criminals who mistook him for a wealthy businessman? I grew up with the impression that we were so much alike that Paulinho, black and a man, was me; we were a single soul in two bodies.

Is it possible to reveal to others, as truth, what our most private feelings see? The same image, just as the same person, can be sad or happy, good or bad, depending on our point of view. The heart has a memory. Sometimes it's called longing, sometimes, resentment. My passion for Paulinho distorts the image I have of him as much as my rancor for Eduardo. My fascination with one discerns as little as my grief for the other. That's why, in a story in which the two blend together, I'm not impartial enough to figure out the objective angle from which others can see the truth in my heart.

I think about what could happen to me if Paulinho were to reappear one day, as in the stories of the return of those thought to have died in war. I look at the example of Berenice, who never forgot her old boyfriend Zé Maria and, even after his marriage, still holds out the hope that one day he will realize his mistake and return. But of the two, Paulinho and Eduardo, the one who exists for me, in flesh and blood, is unfortunately only Eduardo, who sends me news and asks mutual friends about me. No matter how much I want to erase it, his memory still bothers me and is refreshed each time I flip through my diary.

Then I have a flash, a vision: my story should be an innocent vital activity, as if I were erecting a new spiritual house with old bricks, just one, that would shelter my entire past. It won't be a diary, but a book about my present in motion, in which the boundaries between past and future are erased. A present in motion until the end of my days. That's when I develop the theory of instantaneism, whose premise is simple: reality, consisting of body and spirit, is the present moment. Truth only exists completely in the moment.

Unlike Funes, the Memoirist, the Borges character who forgot nothing and remembered everything, I am going to cross my River Lethe to forget everything, to have the freedom to think and write spontaneously, guided only by desire. I will put aside the future, so that I don't construct illusions or predict disasters, which, rather than avoiding them, may even accelerate them. I want to capture the moment, to start from zero. Without any baggage from the past. Without history, without direction. I want to erase myself. To immobilize myself. To condense my life into an instant, to live entirely in it, of it, just like my dog Rodolfo, here at my feet. The instantaneous present. A moment prolonged, like a blurred picture or like frame after frame of a film that doesn't stop rolling. Zero, the moment in which I write, one step from the abyss and from paradise. With me it often happens: I see a single thing as both the promise of heaven or hell. In the blink of an eye, what is light becomes dark. Everything here depends on a moment, hangs by a thread that can be anything from the tenuous line that separates life from death to my mood or some insignificant nothing.

I'm going to rely on the revelation I've had – I think ultimately this is what it's about, a revelation – to take the great leap. Sometimes it's better to have the courage to start over, to discard. Even loves. I'm not one to keep things that torment me. That's why I need to rid myself of Eduardo once and for all. If I can manage to restart from zero, I'm also fulfilling the promise made at that gathering thirty years ago. And the other Useless? Will they make a similar effort at spiritual renewal?

The smoke from the cigarette rises from the ashtray like a chimney. Rodolfo looks at me out of the corner of his eye, surely suspecting that I have gone soft in the head. He lowers his head onto his paws, furrows his brow and lets his sad look become lost in the infinite, a more concrete infinite than mine and on a level with the floor.

I say that all of this "happens" now and not "happened" one day, because I want to describe this instantaneous presence that is always in motion and is defined by it, leaving the endless blotchy stains that I mentioned; I want to show the inside of the moment. The instantaneous present tense of things past. After all, the past is only the trail of an instant, at any instant.

So? In this instant I think that I will live aimlessly, simply traveling within myself. The important thing in life is not just to reach a goal, to arrive at a place, but to enjoy every moment. Because the world doesn't stop spinning, the nature of the journey is more important than its destination. My fears and projects have nothing to do with objective reality, because I'm bewildered and I've already lost all sense of objectivity. I have no interest in knowing what is real beyond the perception of an instant, that catches a look of surprise or pain, a furrow in my brow, my right shoulder contorted, my body unbalanced, fright raising my left hand, while, as in a painting by Caravaggio, my right hand hovers tensely above the boughs and fruits strewn on the table, my middle finger pointing down, from its tip hanging a greedy lizard that bites me. To the side, the water jar in the painting's right hand corner is quiet and translucent, drops visible on its surface. It contains a camellia and its stem, sister of the one I wear in my hair.

Looking at the sheets of still blank paper, I feel that truths are deposited in larvae of words, awaiting even the most banal and unexpected situations, that can bring them together to give them substance and meaning.

After many shaky nights, in which the state of my health only deteriorates, I make a startling discovery. The idea comes to me when I think about the relief of not having to read so much disturbing news ever since Berenice stopped buying newspapers. My new task will certainly give me pleasure for months on end. It's not only newspapers that I don't need. I make the decision to sort the mountain of books, letters and other papers accumulated throughout my life, with the intention of transforming them, as if I were a mill, into a floury mixture of words, that I will then put – all of it – into the same sack. Just having this idea makes me feel light and satisfied and I can finally continue my story. I turn on the stereo, and listen to the lively CD that Jeremias gave me as a gift and I even dance, alone, like a crazy woman, to celebrate an I don't quite know what that unblocks my mind and my soul. Fortunately, only Rodolfo witnesses this state of exultation, and he even enjoys watching my movements.

Not that I had a brilliant idea or even invented something, I know. Ever since the Sumerians, five thousand years ago, invented their writing to record messages, register facts and thoughts in a permanent way... Ever since the Semites, almost four thousand years ago, created their alphabet, the father of almost all of the world's alphabetical systems, writing can be erased, transformed and lost. Ever since language came into existence sixty thousand years ago, tongues have been able to eat tongues and also to preserve the moment forever.

The method will be as follows: I will replace the absence of the papers that I tear up, with new words that I will be writing on blank sheets of paper. This way, I will leave a pain on one sheet, a joy on another, on another grief and sadness. From the books it will be enough to extract what was retained in my memory. I want to free what weighs it down.

In fact, memory is a filing cabinet with closed drawers. Some of the keys to the drawers are made of people, objects, things around us, letters, photographs, and books. Each letter, each one of them, opens an enormous drawer of memories that would perhaps stay closed forever if the letter were not there, physically exhibiting its sentences. By destroying each letter, I will be opening one of these drawers, thereby multiplying the possibilities of the writing of my farewell narrative that I intend to continue composing little by little, a paragraph here, another there.

To become naked and light, free myself of the papers, be reborn free of the weight of the past, is all that I want. With faded ideas it's difficult to avenge myself on sleeping words. Nevertheless, the papers are going to scream, to weep as they are ripped up, restoring life to the ideas and sentiments stored in them. From now on, my instructions are: nothing kept, nothing saved. The moment to dispose of everything I have been accumulating has arrived. And also the moment to free words from their blocks – of granite – made from the emotions time has silenced. Let them emerge, like sharpened knives, sculpting the spirit of the instant. I want to live as in a hypertext that never stops constructing itself, in which writing is a continuous and unending dialogue with the mind or a counterpoint for life. I want to erase all of the books, to allow the natural book to shine, alone: the one they believed in Yucatan, that wasn't written by anyone, that turns its own pages, opening each day to a different one, and because it's alive, bleeds when they try to turn its pages. My interior revolution depends on the courage to continue composing the text, always in the present, while I dispose of accumulated papers. The absent papers will increase my space of freedom.

Seeing my cleanup, Berenice complains:

– Please forgive me, Miss Ana, but it's crazy to get rid of your papers.

– You may throw them in the trash, Berenice.

– You're making a mistake, mark my words.

– Then leave them all there in a pile. I'll decide later.

It's better to make an enormous pile of paper anyway. For example, I can temporarily put in a pile in one corner everything that has to do with love. Despite having mistreated me so badly, love deserves my consideration after all because it contains all virtue. The love pile will perhaps make me see differently than what life has taught me, or simply confirm in the end that I can't have the impossible, that is, the other who measures up to my dream.

I'm going to clear shelves, empty the house, beginning with the room to be rented perhaps to Norberto himself. The papers that bother me are so much a part of my life that the only way to discard them is to transform them into the flour of words I mentioned, sparse dense flour, pounded until it becomes a stone book, a book of life that is as simple and mysterious as a stone.

It will be my version of the *Livre Absolu* that Mallarmé tried to write at the end of his life and finally destroyed before he died. Or perhaps the one quoted in Borges' short story, "La biblioteca de Babel," which completely encompasses all other books. Writing it should help to free me from the books in my library and from the accumulated papers – letters, notes, poems, pages and pages of diaries and other writings. It will be my *museum of everything, dumpster or file cabinet*.

I'll begin the struggle, then. And from the start this is my odyssey of many waves and currents, in which I face winds and storms in an infinite sea, a sea of many encounters, where I travel alone. Alone with my papers and my pen.

I write with the same style with which I live, in other words, as the mood strikes me. I lose ideas in the middle of the path and include in the text whatever comes to mind, without discipline. I have nothing to lose. Only words. And how good it is to discard words and still be capable, as in a factory, of producing others. Holding onto words excessively, protecting them, makes it difficult not only to expand on the text but on my very life.

Passing from theory to practice, I look for the file of correspondence from Eduardo. My absolute priority is to rid myself of him. I should disinter everything that remains of him in order to transform it too into this new flour: in addition to letters, loose sheets with my notes, drawings and also poems. Destroying these papers will make me forget him once and for all. Then, the pain that continues to throb after so many years will finally stop. And what if I were to write to him, returning his letters? Eduardo is much more than one drawer among these papers that I want to destroy. My fingers stain yellow from so much smoking while I flip through the folder. I continue to separate the papers while I review my life with Eduardo, as in a novel. There's no better test for my project. If I manage to rid myself of this folder and am still able to record, in a few words, what I can best extract from my experience with him, I will be successful.

There was a time when I admired Eduardo. But I came to the realization that my love for him was less and less sufficient. Either I was crazy in love with him, or I thought that I didn't love him. Either he wept at my feet, in love, or I feared that he didn't love me. After a few years all that remained of the love that we had for each other was only the harsh daily routine. His presence became trivialized. I began to think him uninteresting, absorbed in his banal politics and his business interests. One day I missed him less than I missed solitude itself. And then he began to bother me. He thought only about sex and work, not about tenderness, or love or me. He wanted success; I wanted happiness. When I wanted to burn in the fire of passion, he offered me security.

I had to get out, as if I were escaping from a prison in which I had confined myself voluntarily out of a fear of taking a chance or of being alone because I thought that alone I was nobody. If I had children, I would have waited for them to grow up. I didn't need to wait any longer.

Eduardo was responsible for my state, above all for the end of my love for him. He was guilty even for my having resumed loving Paulinho, my childhood friend, with whom, as a young girl, I had my first pleasure that all of the others would try to imitate. Fate brought us together. I would have no other reason to love him except that he was he and I am I. I never forgot him. I always imagined that it would be possible one day for us to find each other again, to live together. That original source was Love with a capital L. There's no objectivity in these things; love was the emotion that was mixed into my childhood with Paulinho. All love had that smell, that light, that heat, the pleasure of those same physical contacts.

When I found Paulinho again, I thought only of him. It was an obsession that even caused me to lose weight. I feared that he didn't feel the same way. I accepted the risk, perhaps because it wasn't a matter of choice. I was in love, and nothing diminished my desire, not even my fear of the ridiculous. They say that passion that doesn't end isn't passion, but what I felt for Paulinho wasn't like a passing fever. It was like a fire sparked by the never-extinguished embers of a young love. Despite that, it was truly passion; I recognize it by my suffering.

During Carnival, he sent word that he was waiting for me at the country house. I didn't confirm that I would meet him, but, when I found out that he had disappeared, I even imagined, out of pure spite, that Eduardo had murdered him and that he would be capable of killing me. I ended up denouncing him, stupidly, without any proof.

The worst thing that could have happened to Eduardo was to be called a cuckold. And he was. In public, in newspapers, in magazines, even in a book by a journalist from Brasília. What's worse, he was seen as a meek cuckold. He wanted to get back together; I was the one who refused. I was wounded by some of his words. There's no antidote in the dictionary for certain words that hurt forever. He still thinks about me, after everything that happened and everything I did; he might even leave Alaíde for me, if he knew I was willing.

I had to marry to learn what it is to have a man at my side. In return, I learned that a husband and wife were not made to understand each other. Before, I imagined that there was no happiness without love. Later, I discovered there's no happy love. Once we corrected the youthful error of thinking it was possible to change one another, I was convinced that love is, in fact, a brief insanity, and marriage a long folly.

I'm pleased with the ease with which I rid myself of the papers in Eduardo's folder, without even feeling the need to transpose a single word from them for my story. These are good omens for my project. Until I find a passage, apparently of no importance, written soon after the wedding. It's funny and describes a dream. I'm at a party; the house is Joana's, not her real house, but rather an enormous house with a garden overlooking the sea. I'm on the verandah, like the verandah of a Minas Gerais estate, where several hammocks sway in the wind. I wave to the people scattered around the garden where I see the incandescent red of the geraniums shining under the sun. I'm attractive, wearing a black muslin dress. Inclined over the balcony, I continue watching the movement of the guests and then come the scenes that I would rather not tell. It's enough to say that I can't manage to destroy this sheet of paper already yellowed by twenty-five years of abandonment. Why? Because, as opposed to the other sections of the diary full of complaints, this one leaves me happy. It even makes me laugh, remembering how alive I was and bringing back the memory of Cadu.

2

LOVE, THAT WORD

Everything in Brasília can be seen at a glance. In the clear skies and generous light, the eye sees not just the horizon in the distance but also the dividing line between the city and the countryside. Predictable contours, expected curves. Behind this wide-open light and the evidence of what is planned, a mystery nevertheless persists.

Norberto is on his way. I wrote to him that if he is really convinced he wants to return he can stay with me "for a while." I purposely leave unspecified how many weeks or months.

I still feel weak due to my health problems. At first I attributed my mechanical and romantic inspiration to destroy and produce words to a supposed, but fortunately overcome, consumptive condition. Later the hypothesis arose that I had been contaminated by a multi-resistant bacteria. Finally they diagnosed a virus – common in Brasília – for which the treatment is patience.

I am in the bedroom that will be Norberto's, sorting papers to take to my room, when I hear the noises. Since it's Saturday, Berenice asked for the day off to spend the weekend with Pezão, in the Bandeirante Settlement. Formiga and Vera went to a party. It might be them returning, only there is no reason for them to come in the back door. Then someone forces the bedroom door. Rodolfo, who doesn't move for anything, manages a bark.

I instinctively grab the revolver, my nerves already shattered. I look through a gap in the window: an armed kid. I think about pulling the trigger. The image from the dream appears, the bullet striking the boy's head and the blood spewing. Just imagining that blood I become dizzy, tremble all over, and break out in a cold sweat. Another boy runs behind a porch column with a switchblade in his hand. Maybe they both only have knives, it's impossible to see.

As sometimes happens, suddenly Diana takes control of me. Here I am and am not myself. I was never brave like this. I never acted on impulse, without thinking about what I'm doing. The idea that a revolution is occurring in my life makes me feel prepared to kill or to die. When three guys run by – now there are three – I fire all five of the gun's bullets. I don't know where the bullets will land. I hear a cry of pain from one of them. Another turns toward me, I see him right in front of me:

– You're going to be sorry, bitch!

How could he know that it was a woman who fired? Only if he could see my long hair through the crack.

Courage is a moment of insanity; then come the knots in the stomach. I continue to shiver and sweat; I think I'm going to die of a heart attack. The doorbell rings. It's Carlos, who heard the shots. I open the door panting and with revolver in hand. I am still panic-stricken and accept an invitation to go to his house while I wait for my niece and nephew to arrive. Carmen seems even more frightened than I am.

With his deep calm voice and the smooth gestures of his muscular arms Carlos tries to calm me.

– Let's call the police – he says.

I feel even more afraid.

– The police, no, never. What for? – is all I answer.

Chicão's phone doesn't answer. Berenice, whom I located through one of her neighbors, promises to bring Pezão immediately to repair the door. That way I'll be able to sleep easier.

She ends up coming without her son. Carlos is the one who helps me block the door with my furniture. Then he pronounces yet another of his soccer metaphors:

– Play the tough shots, advance the ball, winning spirit.

I sleep with the loaded revolver under my pillow.

– It would be better to tell the police, because of the threat – Carlos tries to convince me again the following day. – I'll go with you to the station.

– There's no point in telling the police. Even Carmen agreed with me. And what's more, it sends a signal; some corrupt officer will know that sometimes I'm alone – I ponder, as if this were a rational argument; I can't just tell Carlos that I panic at the thought of the police.

I keep mulling over the perhaps foreshadowing dream, in which I confront the bandit who will come to take revenge on me now, that blood spewing from his head... It was my punishment. Hadn't I been asking fate for a revolution in my life? What I really wanted was to win the lottery... And it was a waste for Berenice to buy all those tickets.

Shocked by the attempted robbery, I decide to move to Taimbé. Not right away. I have to sell the house and buy a small apartment where I can leave the kids. First I want to fulfill the promise I made to Norberto for us to celebrate the new millennium together in Brasília.

Close to winter, when he arrives laden with suitcases and stories, I explain these plans of mine to him. Seeing him again is an intense experience. The visual shock leaves me momentarily mute. It's also difficult to adjust to his new name; I'll never be able to call him Berta, much less Helena.

– I've changed, I've changed, I've changed! – he tells me with an affected voice, while still at the airport. He talks like a chatterbox. Full of quirks, he has a happy and enjoyable way of expressing himself, perhaps because the words are accompanied by an incessant gesticulation of lips, face, head, shoulders, hands...

– I don't want to see anyone as Norberto, ok, Aninha? The only exception will be the reunion of the Useless. Even there, let them recognize me.

I am caught between distress and surprise by this Norberto with the high-pitched voice. Berta is a big woman. S/he would be attractive if not for the excessive makeup in addition to the neck and hands of a transvestite. The hair sweeps up stiffly. The dress falls to mid-calf. Two strings of a gold necklace lie over the large silicone breasts. Only one of the two holes in each ear contains rubies. I notice the size of the red shoes: at least a size eleven.

Rodolfo makes a fuss as if he recognized Norberto. Then I show him the painting he did thirty years ago.

– Terrible! It looks nothing like you, because you don't age, right, Aninha? I painted you ninety years old! How did I ever agree to do this? Anyone looking at you now wouldn't say you were even thirty. What a crazy idea, wasn't it? Painting old age… I don't know why you still keep this trash. I hope that it's because it sealed our friendship. I choke up just thinking that might be why. You know, I never painted anything else, just the town – he wiggles his wrists. Then he assures me in a comforting tone: – Look, don't you worry about me, ok? As soon as I get a job I'll rent a place for myself. But I give you my word of honor that I'll help you prepare the reunion. I already have a thousand ideas, you know? We'll talk later. We could have a big New Year's Eve gala at a club, what do you think?

I prefer not to discuss this subject so soon after his arrival. New Year's Eve at a club, over my dead body!

– This is my old friend Berta – I introduce him to Berenice this way, making an effort to refer to him in the feminine.

– I have heard a lot about you, ma'am.

– Don't call me ma'am, you hear? You'll make me feel old.

Berenice just laughs while she takes the three suitcases to the back bedroom, which is the best one because of the separate entrance.

– I put bars on the window and these two crossbars on the door – I show Norberto, so that he's not afraid to sleep in the room of the attempted break-in.

From one of the suitcases he removes a Chinese figurine – potbellied and blood-red. Then he predicts the future, like a fortune-teller:

– It's going to bring you luck. And above all bring you money.

I open a bottle of champagne and propose a toast:

– To your new life!

– To our friendship! – he replies.

Later Chicão arrives bringing his great big voice into the house:

– Wow, you're the same. Exactly the same – he ironizes.

– Don't talk to me like that, you hear? You're the one who hasn't changed a bit; you're still a shit – Norberto retorts, with his hands on his hips, a learned gesture by someone who wants to look like a woman.

Chicão whispers in Rodolfo's ears while rubbing his head:

– Valentino, don't disappoint me. Next time, do like a good Fila: eat the thief – to which Rodolfo replies by wagging his tail for joy.

I pour Chicão some champagne.

– To our reunion – he says, raising his glass.

– You must want to know, right Chicão, why if I could have stayed there, I came back. It's because...

– It's because despite all this mess, this is still the best country in the world! – Chicão interrupts.

– No, it's because to stay there I'd have to become an American. For practical reasons, you know? I have a green card, which is very hard to get. If I married an American woman I would get citizenship. But besides taking a long time, it's too late for that. I just don't know if I'm going to adjust to Brazil, you know? I left in '85 when life here was hard. That wasn't even the reason I left. It was more that I wanted to get lost in the world, you know? I decided to risk it. Portugal, France... And then, about five years ago, the U.S. I had some friends there who even as illegal aliens earned much more than I did... Well, that's the past, right? What I need now is a name. If I had documents as a woman I'd be happy for the rest of my life. That's why I thought of Helena's, you know? Because now I have a new body, a new soul and even a new profession.

Chicão tamps the tobacco in his pipe, with Rodolfo always at his feet (Rodolfo adores him because he always gives him food; forbidding does no good).

– What profession, huh, Norberta? – he asks. For months on end it's like that, he calls him Norberta, to hear the same complaint: "Not Norberta, please…"

Then Norberto explains:

– Most recently I was giving massages. Here, I don't know. I haven't decided yet where I'm going to settle. I heard that Fortaleza is awesome. But, if I find a job, I'll probably pitch a tent right here; I like the oddness of this Brasília. Don't worry, ok, Aninha? It's like I told you, I don't want to be any trouble.

Chicão had heard me say that when she got home the night of the attempted robbery, Berenice had planted herself in front of the door praying aloud.

– I need that prayer – he asks Berenice.

– You don't fool around with these things, Mr. Chicão – she answers, but soon returns with a sheet of paper.

Norberto also wants a copy.

– We never know when we might be in a desperate situation – he predicts.

– You know that despair is one of those five "d's" of Brasília – Chicão remarks.

I say nothing; I think to myself that I've already been through the first three: dazzle, disillusionment, and divorce.

It's a prayer to Saint Judas Thaddeus. On the day of the robbery, Berenice had asked him to protect our house against all danger. "You believe in it, don't you, Miss Ana?" she asked me. "It's good for you to pray, Berenice," I answered. "Always pray. Whether I believe or not is my problem. You are right to pray. Only just now this praying out loud is making me sick."

Facing the champagne and the glass picture window that looks out over the lake, we talk and talk about little nothings. Eventually, Norberto again raises the subject of Helena:

– Tell me everything you know about her. I want to get into her life. Or better yet, to be her.

– For that, first you need to understand every fucking detail of the underground struggle. Have you ever heard of the Marighella

Group? Of the National Alliance for Freedom? Of MR-8? If not, there's no way – Chicão advises. – And what if Marcelo's theory is right, and Helena one fine day disembarks from Cuba or Sweden? – He makes semicircles delicately in the air with his pipe while Rodolfo's head follows the movements of his hands.

– There are things that we know – I try to dot the "i's". – She was arrested, exchanged for an ambassador, and there are witnesses who say that she went back to the Araguaia guerrillas. She was undoubtedly murdered.

– We don't know for sure – Chicão insists, before a perplexed Norberto – Even when they find the remains, they may misidentify the skeletons.

– The program for our reunion should start by paying homage to her memory – I suggest.

– It wouldn't be suitable for you. I imagine you would prefer the version that Helena is alive and that she is you – Chicão comments to Norberto, who says:

– I want to honor Helena's memory, yes sir! I don't care. Our group is one thing; the rest of the world is something else entirely. I wouldn't lie to you, right? I just think that we should also include Eva and the Philosopher in this memorial.

After Chicão leaves, I comment to Norberto about my project to destroy papers.

– What a crazy idea! – he protests.

I show him the chaos in my bedroom.

– Do you understand now? The first order of business will be to destroy those letters and notes. Each discarded piece of paper gives me a feeling of relief and freedom.

– I arrived just in time. I'm not going to allow you to do this. Not over my dead body – he says, with the recurring gesture, hands on waist.

– I don't have room for forty-five cardboard boxes any more. Most of the papers are more than thirty years old. They'll never be good for anything. This box here, for example, is from Taimbé still.

He wants to see Helena's documents. On the envelope it just says "documents" written in her hand. Norberto looks at the folder with respect:

— These days everyone has to belong to a group. Helena was like that. She was a person who belonged to a party, to this and that… I never was.

After he goes to bed, I decide to stay up all night destroying papers and writing pages of my story, now on my laptop. I feel a small twinge of satisfaction when I open one of the boxes. From the pile of letters kept since I was twelve I remove one at random, as someone who expects to be rewarded. First I think about shredding it without even seeing what it is. It's a letter from Rui; I was twenty-seven and because a friend had brought news of him from Florianópolis I sent him one of my poems, published in a small unimportant magazine. Rui, ugly… ugly, no, horribly ugly, despite the large muscular body. He wrote me this letter, a true declaration of love that I never answered. He spent years inventing ways to win my affection. Rui's was a typical Platonic love… I only see him every ten years and I still have no interest in him. But just as with the description of the dream about Cadu, I don't have the courage to destroy the letter. I still want to have the pleasant surprise of rereading a letter like this one, reminding me I was loved, even if by a man as ugly as Rui. Perhaps I should have married him. He would be tender, faithful; he would always be available for me, always notice my clothes, bring me breakfast in bed and do whatever I asked, like not leaving the bathroom floor wet, not leaving newspapers all over the living room floor or whiskey glasses on the table, Eduardo's habits. I plot a chance encounter with Rui. He's still single and he thinks I'm beautiful… We'd probably even be sexually compatible. A man's sensuality can't be measured by the beauty of his face and…if I tried hard, the harshness of his face molded by adolescent pimples and his potato nose have a certain masculine charm. Rui visited me right after my separation. At the time I was in no condition to think clearly, besides being convinced of the advantages of living alone. When the date gets closer, I will send him a birthday card.

Over the following days, I try to accelerate the process of ridding myself of the papers, because I want to empty Norberto's room once and for all. I do it over his and Berenice's protests. There are boxes and more boxes. Here even my friends and ex-friends are classified. I pull them out one by one. And they go into the trash also. Except Norberto, for now, who in fact occupies little space in my files and whose letters I set aside, together with the two pages that I could not bring myself to destroy: the one from Eduardo's folder that describes the dream, and Rui's letter.

Norberto's presence will be good for me. I'll have someone to talk to. He is the extraordinary and revolutionary something that I was expecting. He raises my spirits. He's happy, good-humored and laughs at himself.

Soon after his arrival, Lia has a litter of kittens. It's late one night. We – he, Berenice, Vera and I – go to the laundry room. There we stay until the kittens are born. A litter of six. They're not all the same color. Some are gray, others yellowish. One of the yellow ones is born with white paws. I'm happy. It's as if my life had a new beginning with the arrival of the kittens and Norberto.

He and Vera initially give me the impression that they get along because they can't stop talking. But before she goes to her room she whispers to me in the hall:

– You'll forgive me, Aunt Ana, but this friend of yours is a ridiculous transvestite.

I censure her:

– We can't judge people with cheap eyes of the moment, Vera. We need to have some perspective, and above all, respect. It's like I was reading a few days ago: a cathedral should not be seen up close, because then one sees only the holes in the walls.

– A cathedral? – she asks, with an ironic smile on her lips. – Relax, I didn't see any holes in the walls.

A few days later, Norberto is already naturally Berta to me. She and I are sitting outside in the sunny garden while the manicurist does my nails. The sky is freshly painted a uniform blue without a single blotch. A gentle breeze cools the air. We decided to keep one of the kittens that is playing here. Berta chose the prettiest one, the one with the four white paws. Marcelo wants one for Marquinhos, Jeremias was interested in another, and the others Berenice will take to the Bandeirante Settlement.

I look at the lake, trying as usual to see the projection of the day's colors. It's winter in Brasília, the dry season. I see only the projection of the absence of clouds. I look at Berta's features. Frank. Transparent. In them I still discern the typical native of Brasília, at once savage and gentle. She talks non-stop, hides nothing from me, and is not even intimidated by the presence of the manicurist.

– The visa for the United States was complicated. I bought it in Espírito Santo when I came on vacation for a visit, from a guy who gave me his word of honor that it was authentic. I paid a fortune with borrowed money. When I arrived and showed my passport to the police I was arrested and then deported. I had to return by way of Mexico. I crossed at night through a tunnel and caught a barge. I lost everything: money and even my suitcase. The coyotes themselves were undoubtedly the ones who robbed me. I thought it best not to complain. If I disappeared who would know? Six months later I was living in San Francisco's Mission district. When there was an amnesty I finagled some grapepicker's papers from a vineyard to get my green card. It wasn't very legal but it worked.

Turning to the manicurist:

– What color nail polish do you think I should use, anyway?

Without allowing her to answer, Berta says:

– Now I buy women's magazines to know how to dress, but these things, Aninha, require experience. I very much need your feminine advice. Where do you buy your clothes? More importantly, where do you buy lingerie? Because I don't know the labels here anymore, you know.

Finally, she says:

– I have this son who lives in Guará. It's the first time we're going to meet; I never saw the boy, even when he was born. A delicate situation. His mother is Carolina, who was my girlfriend. A nice girl, you know? I was the one who didn't do right by her. But

I wrote to her two months ago and I received a nice answer with photos of Luís – his name is Luís and he's a journalist. The only thing she doesn't know about is my operation. I thought it better not to tell her in the first letter, you know? I'm just afraid that the boy will be ashamed of me – well, boy in a manner of speaking; he's already grown up. It will be strange for him to call me dad, don't you think? And it's also complicated for him to call me mom, since he already has one.

The manicurist rolls her eyes. I'm not shocked anymore by Berta's stories. To the contrary, I feel well, as I haven't in a long time, being able to open up to a friend on a variety of subjects. Although we haven't seen each other in a long time and this person before me is physically so different from the person I knew, she still inspires my confidence. Berta fell from the sky, from this enameled blue sky. I need someone I can unburden myself to, share my sorrows, joys, fears, hopes, suspicions with, releasing what crushes me inside, and no one better than she, who is not prejudiced, someone to whom even the absurd seems banal. For the worst possible situations she always imagines positive outcomes. This is the definition of a girlfriend, someone to share painting your nails, eating, sitting in the garden… I am only someone when there's somebody by my side making me feel like myself, someone interested in what I am, not in what I have or do. I need someone to confirm that I exist, that I think. I have a friend, Berta; therefore I exist.

– If my son doesn't accept me, I'll understand – she continues.

But her worst fear, she tells me, is actually to continue being a man, a man who had surgery, a man who became a woman, nevertheless still a man: impossible to become a respected professional woman.

– If I at least had my documents as a woman… – she complains.

Then she parades before us, swinging her hips, and hiking her ass:

– Do I really pass for a woman?

And the size of her neck? And her hands? And her fingers?

– You are an extremely charming woman – I try to put her at ease.

– No, I'm not, I know. But I try to keep my figure, don't I?

She takes hormone injections to get curves, full breasts and a round ass. Why don't we exercise together every day?

Actually, if not for her neck and hands, no one would notice that Berta is a transvestite. She's more feminine than I am. But then!? She's taking an intensive course in how to be a woman. She devours every women's magazine in sight.

I don't think it's right, however, that she wants to pass for someone who's dead – or worse, still alive, if Marcelo's version is true. It would be irresponsible on my part to give her Helena's documents. I set them aside with the intention of sending them to Maria Antônia who can include them in a book about the guerillas, send them to an exhibit… She told me once: "Those Araguaia bones will break their silence yet."

Over time, among the prerogatives that I let Berta take over is to decide the menus for meals with Berenice. Berenice doesn't like it. "Don't be difficult," I complain. The result is that Berenice asks for a raise. She claims that her salary hasn't increased in a long time, which is true, and that now there's more work. I explain that I can't give her a raise because the paltry sum I make is shrinking and my expenses have increased. We're both dissatisfied.

Berta and I establish a routine. Together we eat lunch, exercise in the late afternoon, have dinner, and after watching the soap opera, discuss the day's misfortunes. She goes out and I wait for her, taking notes as I tear up my papers. When she returns, sometimes very late, she lies on the bed next to me. I like her presence there. Then Berta tells me, without going into details, one of that night's adventures, in general a come-on from some man she frequently describes as "hot" or a "hottie." I see her as an adolescent exploring the dating scene, more adolescent than Vera.

The fact that Berta had been Norberto helps me feel comfortable around her, but my friendship for her grows more easily than if it were for him. She shows me the value of true friendship: unselfish, expecting nothing in return. I can confirm what has been said about friendship: with Berta at my side my joys are doubled and my sorrows halved.

– Without a husband we don't have anyone to complain to about life; so that leaves friends. Let's promise to always listen to each other – I propose.

– But like true friends, ok? We can tell each other everything, absolutely everything. Promise?

– I promise, under one condition: that we be like psychoanalysts for each other, who have to accept everything we hear and keep professional secrecy.

Each of us has her own life. We don't ask each other indiscreet questions. We like to talk about ourselves and to hear what the other has to say. My ideas become clearer in a half-hour conversation with Berta than in two days buried in my books and papers. One of her suggestions or opinions – sincere and unpretentious – is worth more than a treatise. Berta sees many people. I, however, only talk on the phone with a few of my former university colleagues (mainly Jeremias, despite his annoying nature, who, ever since Chicão's dinner, calls me from time to time) and I see them in this or that little dinner that I can't avoid. It's a relief not to waste time in minor power struggles and to have freed myself from the competition, envy, and intrigues provoked by the work environment.

– We are the perfect couple. Better than if we were married – I confess to Berta in a playful tone, seriously convinced of the advantages of this asexual life. Since she is only sexually interested in men there is no danger of misunderstandings. With mutual respect we do not feed jealousies or place demands on each other.

– You're my sister. You'll always be my sister – she answers me.

We could head a single family that would include my niece and nephew and her son, the two of us taking on the roles traditionally filled by a father and mother.

– You have more luck than sense – I say when she tells me about a visit she made to her former girlfriend Carolina and her son Luís.

– You don't mind, do you? I used you as bait to get him to come over soon. His eyes sparkled when I said that I live with you. He wants to meet you; he thinks you're great… And there's more: he wants to interview you.

– Never – I protest.

I don't know if Berta needs me. I need her. She's the partner I never had. My relationship with Eduardo was always antagonistic. I was never ever to figure out for sure whether he loved me, despite what he said. The more I avoided him and distanced myself, the more he externalized his domineering aggressive temperament and placed non-stop demands on me. I wanted a man who would take care of me, admire, and respect me. But we fought over domestic power as if it were the throne of Napoleon or Queen Victoria. He thought he could boss me around. Sometimes it was a silly thing, we went out for lunch and he wanted me to serve him. When I requested the same thing he refused, he said that I wanted a submissive man. I felt like I was his slave, getting the groceries, running the house, and taking care of his things. In arguments I always lost, he had an answer for everything, I felt humiliated and my voice disappeared. Little by little I was drying up, my emotional life in ruins.

And Berta is sweet to me. We don't compete for anything. We only exchange kindnesses.

She also helps me in family crises. One night Formiga arrives with his face bashed, a bloody nose, and bruises all over his body. A gang fight. Berta and I take him to the hospital and then she treats his wounds. We learned from Formiga himself that Pezão, Berenice's son, had also been involved in the fight.

Several nights after this incident I wake up with television images glowing on Berta's cold expression. Sitting beside me she's watching the news.

– It might be your gardener – she says, after hearing that an assailant killed a resident along the lake who tried to resist.

– No, he's no criminal. But those news reports upset me too. I still hear strange noises in the middle of the night. Sometimes they're footsteps, right here close to the house.

– That kid makes a living selling drugs; trust me.

It may be that Pezão in fact supplies marijuana to Formiga. And I suspect worse; I don't even want to think about it. Berenice herself had told me that she feared Pezão was working for a drug dealer, one day he had been knifed twice…

– He's a smart boy, but he doesn't smell like a rose – I admit.

– He's a bad influence on Formiga and Vera, have no doubt about that.

– I really should let him go, also because having a gardener is a luxury that I can no longer afford. He's only here because of Berenice. The truth is I feel sorry for him, you know? Because he really did try to find a job.

– Don't tell me that you are going to keep this lowlife here because his mother works for you. If I were you I would save that money. Leave the garden to me, I love to garden. You can be sure it will be better cared for than ever.

– You won't be here forever. And you already do too much; you've even become my secretary… – I say, alluding to my letter to the Useless that Berta insisted on typing.

I communicate to Pezão that I no longer need his services. As for the garden, the change works well. Berta has the idea to open a plant clinic. People bring dying plants to be cared for. Berta learns even more about plants and this way our garden looks better than ever, almost as spectacular as Carlos', from whom Berta, in fact, acquires many cuttings. As a business it's terrible. But it keeps Berta occupied, since she was passed over in the selection process for two positions as bilingual secretary. She has no experience, and I think her appearance is alarming. I phoned Japona who had just celebrated the opening of another store. He's going to see if he can hire her as a saleswoman. He doesn't promise, because of the economic crisis.

I try to calm Berenice; I promise a salary increase but can't go back on my decision to fire her son. I cry my sincere cry in front of her while, feeling betrayed, she packs her bags and leaves, not without first threatening that I will still dearly regret having taken in Berta.

— Ana, how can you do something like this? — Chicão wants to know.

— The kid may really be a bad influence on Formiga.

— Or vice-versa, right? People are only influenced when they want to be. They're both adults.

— You say that because you're not in my position.

— The problem is the way you made the decision. You could have talked to Berenice. You two got along so well...

Marcelo gives me the numbers of some agencies. I interview several candidates. I can't find a maid who is good, trustworthy, and who doesn't charge more than I can pay.

Berta starts helping me more around the house. She writes the checks, makes payments, gets the groceries, helps in the kitchen, takes care of the garden... The bathrooms, too. "I did this a lot in Europe," she says. Vera and Formiga take over the dishes and the housework. Finally, I arrange for the woman who irons for Marcelo to come once a week and for his maid to prepare frozen dishes for me.

As if life weren't hard enough, one night they call from the police station to say that Formiga was arrested on suspicion of cocaine trafficking. After talking with an understanding officer, I arrange for them to release him. As a matter of fact, they only caught him using the drug along with others — who, indeed, were carrying quantities that could mean trafficking. I have a serious conversation with Formiga. He only pretends to listen. As time goes by, I notice that he doesn't give up his bad company or become convinced that even the use of a small amount of drugs can cause him serious physical and mental damage.

Vera encourages me to fight my growing despondency with physical exercise. I read the health magazine she sometimes buys me. I take daily walks in the area accompanied by Berta and Rodolfo.

Besides all this, Berta and I start running with Vera in the late afternoons three times a week. These are relaxing times when Berta sometimes asks for lessons on feminine skills, especially how to sashay. She walks ahead of us, swinging her body more or less in time with her stride, hands on her waist, and we have to decide how much sway, because it can't be too much, I say, or she'll look like a hussy; and to be a woman, I comment, you don't have to keep your hands planted on your waist. She thinks that Vera sashays better than I do and tries to imitate her. We have a lot of fun with these lessons.

For Vera, the body is everything. I figure that my niece shares our mutual appreciation for materialism, although hers is more concrete than the historical processes that interest me. At least Vera didn't climb on the mystical bandwagon of Japona's daughter, Monica, who goes to a fashionable guru, an Indian passing through who set up camp on Chapada dos Veadeiros mesa.

As I said, dating is her thing. Ever since Luís appeared at the house the first time, I have been fueling the idea that Berta and I might eventually establish family ties. Luís is interested in Vera. Although she won't admit it, it seems obvious to me that the attraction is mutual. This boy raised by a single mother and the son of a man who became a woman has his head on surprisingly straight. I like the boy. Although quite young he is already a competent journalist. Cultured and polite, he is a beautiful light-skinned mulatto who inherited his father's eyes.

– You shouldn't go out at this hour, Aunt Ana – Vera advises me one night when I mention that I am going for a walk with Berta and Rodolfo.

– I just want to get a little exercise, as you suggested.

Her advice gives me a premonition of some danger. I'm tense not just because of my period; also because I still haven't been able to forget the attempted burglary and I never stop hearing stories and more stories about violence. I decide to wear my wristwatch, a little gold chain around my neck, and one hundred reais in my pocket just to give to the thief, if necessary, besides – for the first time on our walks – the gun, that I put in my pants pocket.

I attach Rodolfo's leash and we're off.

– I hope that you haven't regretted letting Pezão go.

– I didn't want Berenice to leave.

– Shit, you don't say. I didn't either. I actually talked with her a lot. She told me a thousand things in confidence. Did you know she had an affair with Cadu, when she was Eva's maid?

A half moon, with the pale light of its violet rays, bathes the silhouettes of the houses, the trees, and the vast dry lawns.

– I feel very lonely. Life is like that, better alone than in bad company. I'm fortunate to have a friend like you. They would never accept me at home – she complains.

– I guarantee they'll jump for joy when they find out you are back.

– No, there's no point in trying; I have given up on two things: I will never be accepted at home and I have no hope of getting married. Flings don't satisfy me any more. What I'd really like would be to find a man who understood me and wanted to live with me. That's not going to come along.

– You're still very young, with your whole future ahead of you.

– My problem is that I was never able to surrender blindly, for my entire life. Once I told a stranger that I was going to love him forever because he was going to be far away and we wouldn't see each other again. A love like one loves a portrait, you know? Something that doesn't change, that has that familiar and expected beauty. But regarding what I want to be my reason for living, I'm afraid of making a mistake. I can't run the risk of making a mistake in love of all things. Surrender to someone I'm afraid of losing? Never! The worst thing is that this didn't keep me from losing the one I loved most, who was also the one I hated most, who most filled me with fear and who I most want to forget.

I imagine a sick relationship, perhaps sadomasochistic.

We walk in silence. Rodolfo is loose and stops at his first tree. He's always had his favorite trees for peeing. He roams among the bushes in the neighbors' gardens while we hear the sound of our shoes on the cement sidewalk.

– It's really neat being your friend, you know? – The emphasis that Berta places on the sentence comes out between an open smile and an affectionate masculine slap on my shoulder.

Engulfed in sweet emotion, a kind of essence of friendship, I make her the following proposition:

– If you're really determined to stay here I'll give up the idea of returning to Taimbé next year. We'll share the house permanently. We can keep each other company.

She doesn't answer me.

– Life for me these days – I continue – is this: letting myself be carried by the tide.

– You have to like living. To like life. Work up some enthusiasm, go out, relax, you know?

– I'm not young enough to go to bars like you. I want to concentrate on what I set out to do. My pile of papers still hasn't reduced the way I'd like.

It's the end of the winter, the height of the drought, but the yellow leaves of the sibipiruna trees tremble under the streetlight. I notice the poinsettias with their red leaves.

– I can only imagine one thing more important to me than my story: money to live on – I speak this half-truth thinking that when Berta gets a job perhaps she can split the house expenses with me; I have to be practical.

At the curve in the path, reflections of the other bank – of fear and apprehension – twinkle over the blade of water in Lake Paranoá. Suddenly I see myself talking about something I don't like and saying something I have never thought:

– Despite everything that has happened, I regret that my marriage to Eduardo didn't work out.

– As always, the one I want doesn't want me.

– That's not it. It was all my doing. It's possible to negotiate an intimacy between two adults or even to guide this intimacy to a love built over time, one helping the other, lending a hand during the tough times, sharing common interests and pleasures. I shouldn't have allowed things to reach that point.

– The problem is that someone else appeared in your life, right?

– A passion like the one I felt for Paulinho was not uncontrollable, irresistible – I surprise myself saying.

Just a few days before I had distractedly and randomly leafed through the pages of my diary. Through them, as one might expect, a whole forgotten drawer of memories had been opened. Registered there in round letters and purple ink was a night of internal peace. My marriage to Eduardo had reached a point of equilibrium, of mutual respect, enveloped not by fire or snow; but by the warmth of affection, so I felt and wrote at the time. I had learned how to control my passions, chase away my fears, and accept my limitations. How naive… How time had fooled me, had deceived me about apparent realities, and swallowed up my brightest dreams into the depths of the seas.

I should at last throw away the pieces of my life I've already forgotten, I thought, while arming myself with the courage to release those sheets of paper over the waste basket. Then I was going to tear them up, or better yet, set fire to them. A painful decision, as if a part of me had been lost. It wasn't self-destruction, but rather an opening of doors when I felt suffocated. Suffocated by something inside myself, by an internal, perhaps imaginary, climate.

– My problem was that I couldn't content myself with the possible – I say. – I suspect that now it is the possible that doesn't come to me. In retrospect, Eduardo was loving and faithful at heart. I was the one who didn't realize it in time to avoid that whole situation that degenerated into heartache, resentment, and violence.

– Dream on. No man is faithful. You must think that I'm not a good example but my periods of promiscuity were due to my masculine side… Because a man has no imagination; he needs experiences. And look: love either exists or it doesn't. If it's dead, it's dead. There's no mouth-to-mouth resuscitation that will revive it.

I understand her point of view; it's not just love that can't be prolonged artificially; it's any sentiment.

– You're right – I say – but loneliness is much worse.

During my marriage to Eduardo I doubted whether the word love corresponded to anything more than an expectation or a quest, to a famished misery, to that absence without which desire cannot exist. But after the separation, in place of these feelings of absence, with time, only a heavy emptiness and a light hopefulness appeared:

that a casual encounter might transform my life… Could I possibly ever get Eduardo back?

The serious moment is marked by the click of our slow steps on the pavement.

– Do you still see each other?

– No, almost never.

– Leave it to me. – Berta breaks into a happy smile. – If you want it to, it will happen; the world belongs to those who know how to fight. – Then she points up. – Look at the moon. – As if she were only seeing it then. – The sun belongs to men; the earth, to women, but the moon is mixed, like me; I identify with it.

– That's already in Plato.

She reacts with the surprised look of someone in doubt.

On the way back we approach the house.

– Perhaps I also need to buy a gun for self-defense – Berta comments.

– Any specific problem?

– No, none, silly! There you go with your paranoia – she beams a reassuring smile. – It's just that it's dangerous to walk alone in the middle of the night.

– It's hard to get a permit to carry a weapon, and you're in more danger than I am. Here, you keep the gun. – I give it to her. – I only ask that when you don't need to go out with it you always leave it on top of the wardrobe in my bedroom.

That's when we see Carlos and for the first time I think that if he weren't married he could very well be the person I seek. He's so nice, so attentive to me. His calm muscular movements communicate security. A man who likes flowers so much must have a good heart. Carlos comes down from the porch to the sidewalk to greet us.

It's eleven o'clock when we walk back in the house. I feel relieved that nothing has happened to us. It was just a foreboding. But I continue to feel anguished, perhaps for having stirred up things I shouldn't have, for having thought about that lack of love, about Paulinho, about Eduardo.

Berta follows me to my room and notices the boxes full of paper all over the floor.

– I'm still in my tearing up phase. I don't know where to start next, there are so many files – I comment.

– I would do it by the date. By the oldest.

I don't know whether she's being ironic, but maybe what she says makes sense. Then she puts the gun atop the wardrobe:

– Today I won't need it.

I vent my anxiety by taking it out on the papers:

– Trash, trash, trash! – I scream when I begin to throw the boxes of paper into the trash. My movements rush toward a crescendo until they completely free my anger. I am free like Diana, free to rage and destroy these words that are stones in my path.

It's the freedom that Berta gives me to be myself, to externalize my eccentric and inexplicable anger, anger at myself.

– My life is trash! – I roar.

I chose this failure myself, nothing that is happening in the outside world interests me, my past ideals no longer make sense…

– I am going through a difficult phase, Berta. Thanks for being here at my side. – Losing control, I start to cry.

It had been a long time since I cried. I didn't know that my eyes could still spill that many tears. Norberto's presence, with Berta's new look, resuscitates me, freeing my sadness. Berta rubs my back with her hand and then hugs me without saying a word.

– The only thing worthy of note in my life is this reunion of ours – I continue while drying my tears. – It's like I said, loneliness is worse.

We go to the kitchen where Berta makes me a cup of chamomile tea to calm my nerves and tries to console me:

– You have your family, your mother, Regina…

– But they don't count. My family is my niece and nephew, you and even Berenice who abandoned me.

– Ana, you're the most intelligent person I have ever met. Whatever you want to do, if you really want, it will work out.

Everyone who meets you is charmed. You are pretty, you're interesting... You're admired, you're respected... So, lighten up, ok?

We take our tea to the living room. I put on some jazz. I listen to Cole Porter with the feeling that I can survive and be happy – whatever that word means – alongside Berta and my niece and nephew.

– You're my best antidepressant – I tease.

Berenice is the only one I really miss, like a dear one who had died. And I laugh to think – could it be true? – of the affair that she had with Cadu, the "sweet fuck", as they called him. Berenice will return one day, like the prodigal son.

Before I go to bed, going through papers as usual, a small sheet with a passage from *The Banquet* and a lot of scribbles falls on the floor: "Hesiod says that what existed first was Chaos, then Earth, the basis for all things, and Love...." Love, that word, the word known to all... Just one word, a simple word, but how many images it continues to provoke in me, of what I lived and mostly what I couldn't live... For now I am going to keep this sheet, leaving it here on the love pile, leaning against the wall on the left side of my bed, a pile that has been growing and will be the last to be destroyed.

3

LOVE'S LABYRINTHS

Everything is reborn in the spring, they say. That's my hope. Late September, it still hasn't rained. The grass is burned in several parts of the city. Only the bougainvillea in my garden with their pinks, purples, and reds resist the inclemency of the climate. Carlos' rose bushes too, the fruit of his special care. There is a desert dryness in the air, a paradise for viruses. The result: I get conjunctivitis and the second viral infection in six months.

But this all changes when I receive the invitation from Jeremias to take part in a roundtable at the university. Although the academic world no longer interests me, I like that he remembers me. To know that someone – even if this someone is Jeremias – considers what I have to say relevant is like receiving an injection of new blood. Maria Antônia, also invited, is coming from São Paulo especially to participate.

Since Regina will bring Juliana to Sara Kubitschek Hospital for surgery, I decide to kill two birds with one stone, applying a method similar to that of my story: at the same time that I take notes for the talk, I will bring the remaining books to my room that are still in Berta's, thus making more space there for another bed.

As in a sacred ritual, I hold each book in my hand and close my eyes while I think about what it taught me. Sometimes only a vague idea remains, in others the title or a sentence that I copy before throwing them, one by one, onto the floor against the wall opposite the one where I threw the papers on love, from where they will next move to the trash. The words had fallen on me like autumn leaves, beautiful and colored, but soon swept away by the wind. The only words that still had meaning were the ones that had been born inside me and had grown like evergreen leaves that never fall from the trunk. I spend several days jotting down ideas in a disorganized way, while I make arrangements with Sara Kubitschek Hospital for the arrival of Juliana, who needs good doctors to correct a mistake. She fell from the top of a tree, broke her leg in two places, and it was set incorrectly.

I spend more time getting ready than practicing what to say. I take a long shower, the bathroom is the room I like most; I built it especially large. I have to look happy, naturally elegant. I curl my hair while I dry it. I lightly pencil my eyebrows. I put a touch of mascara on my lashes. A pale lipstick, nothing heavy. I try on a skirt. Although it's only a little above the knee, I don't want to have to worry about crossing my legs in front of the audience. I'm going to wear my raw linen outfit.

When I enter the kilometric corridor of the Giant Worm, the main building at Brasília University, I still don't know how I'm going to present my disjointed ideas. My sheets of notes are no good, not even for the Three Stooges. Jeremias tells me about his cat, one of Lia's offspring, while Maria Antônia gives me a long hug. She has primped: a cream-colored dress, large hoop earrings, rouge on her dark cheeks, and a big Afro. I notice Chicão and Berta in the audience.

The circus begins. I hear denouncements of several -isms: by a professor from Rio Grande do Sul, against integrisms and fanaticisms; by Maria Antônia, against cynicism, postmodernism and neo-liberalism. I defend my ism: the acceleration of time doesn't allow us any option except instantaneism. I'm not referring to the ideal landscape, where quiet and repose predominate, but to the instant in motion, like in a painting by Klee, or to the motion in the instant, to the immediately visible and to meaning as the instantaneous result and cause of action. "Let us not run from the instant," I exclaim to the audience, putting all my energy into those words.

A speaker wearing a tie agrees with me while vomiting complex concepts to affirm that the space for foresight is gone, substituted by simulations and virtual experiences. He thinks that's all instantaneism is, which irritates me greatly. He points out the advantages of living in real time where space and time are no longer perceived. Little by little there would be calamities that would not have time to occur because they would have already been staged meticulously in the virtual world.

When Jeremias speaks about not spending more than one has, about efficiency, competition and belief in the future, someone in the audience accuses him of being a neo-liberal. The guy in the tie takes Jeremias' side, angering others. The audience becomes excited. The right to work is fundamental, one says. No, the right to leisure is fundamental, people should be valued for themselves and not for the work they do, cries another.

The confusion provoked brings more blood to my head. I unleash words, as I haven't done in some time. It must be old age that by putting me in a state of grace between life and death gives me this freedom. I am inflamed; I am Diana. Everyone follows, not my reasoning, but the light in my eyes and the recognizable passion in my hand gestures and in my tone of voice:

– Everything can evolve in many directions, even those that we don't foresee, and unknown reality is always greater than the dreams we dream. I disagree with whoever says that there is nothing new under the sun and whoever thinks that things aren't done like in the old days. With someone who believes that nothing changes and someone else who, on the contrary, thinks that everything that happens is without precedent.

I use the instant as if it were a sack in which I place several images, concepts, and reflections, even though I know that it escapes and flees from me like a mirage, as I approach it:

– In the instant, plans, dreams, provisions are made; as in stock market values, the highs and lows of obligation and responsibility, morals, and work ethic, are measured along with the capacity to construct something as a team. The instant can always revolutionize tradition – I go on to say, raising my voice and savoring every word of my well-argued rhetoric – nothing is inevitable except the struggle of some against others, of selfishness against solidarity, freedom against tyranny, knowledge against stupidity, of any meaning against its opposites. No reality is immutable, all ideas can be reborn, men can aspire to better ways of life, even when worse ways appear; the world changes instantaneously for the better and the worse at the same time.

And I conclude my presentation this way:

– Just because selfishness won the day against solidarity, we shouldn't throw away our ideals, but collect them in this sack of instants. There is room for ethics in realism.

There is a disheartening silence. Only Chicão asks a question:

– Don't you all think that we are living in the splendor of chaos?

No one on the panel responds. Someone from the audience who says he has read on the subject predicts that after a materialist phase there will be a return to spirituality.

This is definitely not my trip. No students come up to me, no one congratulates me. So that I won't feel too bad Chicão grabs me by the waist and lifts me up as if I were a ballerina while announcing to the four winds:

– You are my candidate for governor!

Jeremias thanks me for my presence in an almost pro-forma way. Another former university colleague thinks he's consoling me by saying:

– You were the only one who didn't stick to a purely technical discussion.

In essence, I feel humiliated.

– I didn't understand anything you said – Berta says.

– But there really isn't anything to understand – I tell her.

Japona had invited us – me, Berta, Chicão, and Maria Antônia –

to dinner at his restaurant at 204 South. A preview, as he had said, of our end of the year reunion. Beforehand, Maria Antônia said she would stop by my house. So I ask Chicão to bring her in the late afternoon, and we'll go together from there.

This afternoon, when Chicão and I go into the kitchen, Berta is seated at the table with Vera (the two have been close ever since Vera went public with her relationship with Luís, a relationship that is very good for Berta, because it allows her to see her son often). I hear the following:

Berta:

– We're having a little girl talk here. I was telling Vera that instead of wearing those tight panties it's better to wear nothing at all. I only wear Calvin Kleins, the bikinis, right? Because the briefs are comfortable but kind of ugly. Or else lace panties in black or white, I don't like any other color. Or the silk Victoria Secrets. I think they're great, soft, super sexy… I don't even mind if they give me a wedgie because I like the ones that leave my butt bare. I don't know what I'll do when my supply runs out; who has money to import more, right?

Chicão:

– Did you know that panties are from the fourteenth century? European courtesans wore them as tools of seduction.

Berta:

– They could only have been invented by whores.

Vera:

– What I don't like are tight bras.

Berta:

– Well, unfortunately I have to wear them, you know? Americans like big boobs, but it was a mistake to want these big implants. Look – he puts his hands underneath making them bounce – they're falling for the second time. I'll give you some womanly advice – looking at Vera – : enjoy your youth while there's time.

– This conversation, as innocent as it might be, leaves me with the impression that Berta exerts a bad influence on Vera. She doesn't even resemble the delicate fellow we knew thirty years ago – I comment to Chicão. In fact, I start to see her as an opaque crystal, falsely transparent, and I remember Berenice warning me that I would yet regret having taken her in.

– You with your moralism again – he answers.

– That's not the only reason. Little things irritate me. A few days ago, she had lost her house keys. Can you believe she emptied her entire purse in front of me on the sofa in the entryway? Exposing your intimate things on the sofa is crude, don't you think? I was shocked. Not shocked by the contents of her purse, which besides a tube of Vaseline was full of the normal things: mirror, receipts, cosmetic bag, lipstick, wallet, mints… More by the act, you know?

– Remember she's still learning to be a woman.

Also this afternoon Maria Antônia gives us some information:

– You already know, right? The government recognized Helena's death. They agreed to issue her death certificate.

– Shit, we can't let that happen – Berta says. – Her remains weren't found – she keeps repeating.

Later, when we're alone, getting ready to go out, she confesses that she had already taken Helena's document file; she had gone back to black hair precisely to resemble her. And she announces categorically:

– I won't allow them to kill me.

– You can't be serious – I react, bewildered.

– I need to go on being Helena. I've already started my new life with her identity. I've made connections. This is my last chance to be somebody…

– But you don't look anything like her, Berta – I observe, trying to put a normal face on an absurd conversation.

– There are many people who don't look like their ID photos…

– And what about your height?

– And since when is height on the ID card? – she asks with a pose that displeases me, hands on her waist.

– It must be on some document.

– Documents can be wrong, can't they? And the eyes are brown, the skin brown, the hair black, everything's the same.

– I know only one thing: you won't just make the news; you'll be arrested, also – I warn her, remembering what Marcelo said about the Penal Code.

She frowns and at the last minute doesn't want to go to dinner with us. She claims some mysterious engagement that can't be postponed.

This is only the second time that I've seen Cassia, Japona's wife. The first was many years ago, when the two of them invited me to Sunday lunch at their house in the North Peninsula.

At the start of the evening Maria Antônia protests because Chicão lights his pipe:

– Cigarettes, all right; but no pipe. We'll all be impregnated with that disgusting smell.

Chicão ignores her and continues to blow puffs into the air while drinking his *caipirinhas*, made, according to Japona, with Salinas ten-year-old *cachaça*.

I notice the copper pots hanging on the walls, the clay pots on a table, a large arrangement of dried flowers and a replica of one of Aleijadinho's prophets carved in soapstone in one of the corners.

Cássia recites the menu, stressing that the spices are authentically from Minas: beef jerky stew; *iaiá-com-ioiô*, she explains, is a ground beef with corn mush; *ora-pro-nóbis*, the green that spices and gives its name to a dish made of beef round; *roupa velha*, pulled beef with rice; *vaca atolada*, which are beef ribs served with boiled manioc. Finally, we all order the dorado fish stew with manioc mush.

Cássia is not from Minas, she's from Goiás. They opened a *mineiro* restaurant by accident. They found an excellent cook from Minas, and so they gave up the idea of a sushi bar.

Japona provokes Maria Antônia:

– Things don't look as bad as you paint them. Some good changes are happening on a small scale.

– Small scale? – she asks indignantly.

– In the little things, here and there – Japona tries to explain.

– More people with initiative. There's no miraculous formula that will change people's lives overnight.

– Not overnight. But being on the left makes a difference, making policies directed at the poor or the rich – she says.

– And can you make policies only for the poor? The economy depends on big industry and large banks – he goes on.

Maria Antônia accuses him with a smile:

– Japona is a conservative now.

And he, serious:

– Perhaps. Many things do need to be conserved. And there are many illusory and wrong changes.

– I really think, you know, Maria Antônia, that the world has changed, you're the one who hasn't changed – says Chicão. – Governments change but you keep fighting against them, any of them. Your thesis is always that everything changes to stay the same and "si hay gobierno, estoy en contra." That's blindness, you know?

– Look, we are never going to agree, basically because you're a son of a bitch who practices cynical reason, while I think that the struggle is worthwhile – she answers.

– The fish is excellent – I say, trying to head off the fight brewing.

– Today it would be possible to eliminate hunger and misery in the world – Japona reintroduces his optimistic view.

– Japona, tell me how to get rich! – Chicão asks, without stopping his drinking, his hairy belly now showing beneath his unbuttoned shirt.

– You're the only one here who lives off his investments – Japona retorts.

– Just imagine, man! – Chicão says. – Marcelo and I made a pact. I only invest in savings accounts that pay nothing. While he, the risk taker, loses a ton of money in risky investments.

– He may not be rich, but he's the only one with powerful friends – Maria Antônia gets in her digs.

– I only make powerful en-e-mies, starting with you – Chicão fires back, between serious and playful.

– I'm neither your enemy nor powerful – she maintains.

– You're the only one here with power, Maria Antônia, you

know that – Chicão says. – Or do you think that the only ones with power are entrepreneurs and people in government?

Ignoring Chicão, Maria Antônia turns to Japona:

– You're right. It would be possible to eliminate hunger and misery. But we don't have an elite capable of standing up to the march of capitalism that's headed in the opposite direction.

– What matters in history isn't the virtue of the elite – Chicão says – but the level reached by the multitudes of the mediocre. If they become educated, have enough to maintain their dignity and even learn a few things about civics...

Maria Antônia interrupts, sharply:

– The problem is also that these bureaucrats do nothing...

Chicão doesn't let her finish:

– It's better to do nothing at all. If you do something, you're screwed. To begin with, doing is expensive. And these days the best administrator is the one who doesn't spend.

– You don't have to be defensive, Chicão. I'm referring to the politicians, who...

Chicão gets angry:

– Shit, all the problems here are the politicians' fault! What I don't understand is this language that "the country is always doing poorly," "it's in a crisis" always, and it's the politicians' fault. The world is imperfect, Maria Antônia, and in motion, get it through your head once and for all! That's why I liked the lecture by my friend Ana here, who understands this, right, Ana? There is no point in which things are doing well. It depends on for whom, in relation to what. There are always things to improve and others to keep. Let each person do his or her part.

– Some people try to reduce the confusion that others want to increase – I timidly continue Chicão's argument.

No one even listens to me. Then I say to Maria Antônia:

– That hairstyle looks great on you! – Truly, I have the impression that she is prettier and younger than in the old days.

She thanks me with a word and a smile, but her interest is more in continuing the argument:

— You're a petit bourgeois conformist – she says to Chicão.

— Now hold on there! – he reacts. – I just think that we already know the ideals. They're never going to be met. It's more useful to reflect (really reflect, not just think that everything is the politicians' fault) on how inequalities arise; how injustice is created; how stupidity proliferates; how political disorder is created; how to beat the best laws and the tax man...

— So now you're interested in usefulness, are you? – Maria Antônia retorts.

— I'm still a dialectic – Chicão says.

— You mean to say an ethylic – she emends.

I seize the moment to explain my theory of the drunken pendulum that actually, I tell Chicão, has to do with the idea of the splendor of chaos and is an addendum to instantaneism. But, in fact, he's drunk.

— The pan... pande... pandemonium here in this country is total – he says, tripping over one of his favorite words. – It's every man for himself and God against all.

— No, God is still Brazilian – Japona affirms, and says that they're both wrong; they're radicals on opposite sides, and they're both allied with inaction. Chicão talks and talks and does nothing; and for Maria Antônia action is only worthwhile if it's impossible.

— That's why we're useless – Chicão concludes.

— Words alone are not enough, emotion isn't either: one has to do something – Japona elaborates his reasoning. – It's better to walk a short distance with real steps than to want to leap with acrobatics. *Everything is worthwhile if the soul is not small.*

— You complain on a full stomach, Maria Antônia – Chicão says.

— And you're a daddy's boy. A typical example of the dominant Brazilian class...

— Fuck you! – Chicão holds up his middle finger.

— You have no character – Maria Antônia continues.

— And you have no balls to play with. You need a man – he answers.

– Look here, buddy. Fuck you! I won't lower myself to your level, ok? You're a shit with no principles, a boring little Fascist, chauvinist, sexist, insensitive...

– Up yours, got it? Up yours! – he yells.

I take Maria Antônia to her hotel. After I drop her off I get that feeling I always do: I'm so afraid as I drive home that I have heart palpitations. I'm panic-stricken when I stop at the garage entrance. I don't even have the gun that's with Berta. I'm vulnerable, delivered up to anyone wanting to rob me. Let them take my car, my purse, and anything else they want. Fortunately, as before, I enter the house unharmed.

Berta arrives late, and when Leo is run over by a car the next morning she's still sleeping. So I go alone with Leo to the vet. In the waiting room, five other people, two with their cats, two with dogs, and a woman alongside me who cries a heartfelt cry as if she had lost her own child. She must be going through a traumatic experience like mine.

The vet tells me that my cat's recovery is not just expensive but almost impossible. We finally decide to put Leo to sleep with a lethal injection. I am devastated. How painful it is to say goodbye to a pet like him! I don't even want to think about the time when Rodolfo's death arrives...

The woman continues to cry on one of the benches in the waiting room, her dark skin, soft curves, a body both Renaissance and indigenous. Her facial features are classic, one might even say Greek. She is disheveled, without make-up. The black dress with the elegant cut makes a low curve down her back and buttons on the side with three pale wooden buttons, the one in the middle absentmindedly unbuttoned. She resembles a character in a tragedy, a strong personality living out her great drama.

– I had to euthanize my cat – I tell her, assuming it's easier to tolerate pain shared in solidarity. – There are moments in life when we have to make difficult decisions. You can't keep one of these dear pets on artificial respiration. My cat was already in a coma, you know? He was in great pain; he wouldn't recover... Is yours a dog or...?

– It's a cat, too – she answers, still crying. – I don't know what to do with him.

– And the vet, what does he think?

– He didn't even see him, I left him at home – she tells me, sobbing.

– And does he have any chance of surviving?

– He's already dead – she says and starts to cry louder, in deep despair.

I don't understand what this woman is doing here, but I'm unable to leave, I stay beside her, trying to console her. Her cat's body is in the refrigerator, only she doesn't know what to do with it. She had come to the vet, a friend, with the idea of getting rid of the body.

– I'll never be able to – she says.

– And a plot in an animal cemetery? – I suggest.

It crosses my mind that if she doesn't want the expense, and the problem is that she lives in an apartment, we can bury it in my garden, plant some flowers that Carlos especially recommends over the grave. I only think it, fortunately I don't say anything, in time to realize the risk of being bothered every week by a stranger in love with her deceased cat.

– I don't want to be separated from Milu – she answers, crying still louder.

– Don't you have somewhere to bury him? – I ask again.

– Yes, I do, but I don't want to. I can't part with Milu – she repeats, still sobbing.

I leave relieved to discover that there are worse calamities in the world than mine.

When I return home there is no longer time to attempt a reconciliation between Maria Antônia and Chicão, or even to say goodbye to her.

– Advance the ball, winning spirit – Berta says to me with Carlos' words.

Days later I meet Marcelo and Chicão by accident in the ParkShopping Mall. The subject is Maria Antônia. Chicão hasn't forgotten the argument they had.

– She's still a fanatic. And fanaticism blinds, you know? Did you know she's black now? – he turns to Marcelo with an ironic smile in his eyes, continually puffing heavily on his pipe.

– Yeah, she's become an activist – I agree with him. – But if her father is white and her mother is black, she can choose, right?

– She's brown – Marcelo says, with an attorney's precision.

– That's exactly what she doesn't want. She prefers a radical definition of color. In the old days it would never occur to anyone, not even her, that she was black. Times have changed – I say.

I return to my regular routine, now with my bedroom impassable, there are so many books and papers on the floor. One night, when I lie down after rummaging through the papers and throwing the notes for the university talk in the trash, I confirm that the spider web that I noticed in anguish so long ago is not only still here; it has grown and occupies a whole corner of the ceiling. And the spider web directs my thoughts to Berenice. It is proof that I see her as the maid I miss, not the friend. I can't deny this is so; I need Berenice to clean my ceiling. The difficulty of living without her grows with the prospect of Regina's arrival with my niece Juliana. Chicão will say that I'm self-centered, but there's no other solution. I need a maid. I need Berenice.

So I ask Formiga to take me to her house in the Bandeirante Settlement. Berta doesn't argue. None of us (including Vera and Formiga) had any confidence in the mission's success, but to our surprise, Berenice accepts my apologies amid tears and remorse. I don't even care that she doesn't talk to Berta. Let them work it out.

With Berenice's arrival, and now freed from a number of daily chores that stole much of my time, I'm finally able to transport all of the papers and books that were still piled in Berta's room to my bedroom. Now they form part of the pile along the right side of my bed that almost reaches the ceiling, ready to be carried to the trash.

In recent months, making this pile, desanctifying words and preparing them for the trash, has been my amusement. I build at least one row of books per day along the longest wall in my room, something concrete that I conquer. I will be fully satisfied when I have eliminated all of this material, not just emptying my room of this trash, but also freeing my mind from so many concepts bound by words laid down throughout my life. Just as matter and anti-matter exist, words and anti-words exist. I will then be capable of discovering anti-words that unspeak or swallow accumulated words. Am I not the very essence of uselessness?

Faced with the almost endless path I must cover, what I accomplish every day, every hour, is palpable, unlearning myself before a wall. Here I live my negative life, the negation of my accumulated words – those that I have read, written, or saved. I still haven't been able to empty my mind. On the other hand, I create space for two beds in Berta's room and prepare myself to receive Regina.

My routine is broken by one more tragic fact. Leo's death still pains me, when Berta brings me the news that Carmen, Carlos' wife, has died of a heart attack.

– There are moments when sorrows pile up – I tell Berta.

– There's a viewing. She'll be buried this afternoon – she informs me.

We decide to go to Carlos' house.

I look up at the sky. It's sad, dressed in dark shrouds, about to pour its tears over the large sweeps of yellow grass stained with gray.

I put on a discreet short-sleeved navy blue dress. I don't wear black only so I don't look like a relative of the deceased.

Berta appears in full make-up and a short strappy leopard print dress that matches her shoes.

– If you go dressed like that I'll pretend I don't know you – I threaten.

– What does it matter to you how I dress, anyway? Tell me. – She puts her hands on her waist, her right foot shaking in a rhythm of threat and demand.

While we argue we head to Carlos' house, and the way that she exaggerates the swinging of her hips in that tight outfit bothers me – she learned nothing from the lessons in moderation that Vera and

I gave her. We go through the gate and then find ourselves suddenly at the entrance to the living room, the coffin in front of us, and the two of us still arguing.

I look to the sides: a dozen strangers bothered by Berta's presence. They have noticed her manly neck and hands. They find that outfit and that overdone make-up odd on someone at a viewing. I think of the dead cat in the freezer. I imagine its owner, the Greek Indian, being here also, completing the strange landscape that I observe like a sleepwalker. Carlos, in dark glasses, with his two children at his side, ignores Berta. He merely acknowledges her. He squeezes my hand hard while thanking me for my condolences.

Carmen's body reminds me that the only thing left for me is decline. And to think that, according to my adolescent calculations, I would already be, if not rich, then at least famous, surrounded by friends and a loving, understanding, generous, attentive man... A terrible black vision of the world surrounds me. I have been devoured by life. I am the most miserable of creatures. A black slave. A destitute and mistreated woman. A street urchin. Landless. A dying Jane Doe in a charity hospital. An unknown pauper's body left to a teaching hospital, then dissected in an anatomy class... I suffer for all the wretched of the Earth. I am Carlos. I feel his pain deep inside of me... Seeing Carlos cry, I cry too, and am ashamed of crying as if I were a family member. My crying has nothing to do with Carmen. I cry for Leo, too soon dead. I cry inexplicably for that desperate woman with the dead cat in the freezer. Mostly I cry for myself, for being aware, ever since the night I cried on Berta's shoulder, of being sad and alone.

Berta returns home still annoyed by my criticisms. In my car, I follow the small funeral procession to the cemetery. I'll wait to talk with her when I return. Among the identical tombs and rows of trees, I follow Carlos, his children and friends. I meditate on the things one meditates on at these moments. My life's emptiness. The uselessness of living. The work that I would like to leave behind in the world. My failure to raise my niece and nephew. The children I never had...

The burial is quick and simple, without solemnities or eulogies. The first shovels of red clay are thrown on Carmen's coffin, already lowered into the grave. The teardrop that rolls down below Carlos' dark glasses moves me. I can't contain my own tears.

The first rain in months falls. I don't know how to explain it, my tears are now tears of joy. The sky is also crying for joy. Pent up energy – in me, in the atmosphere itself – is freed. I have been waiting for this rain for so long... Drops had already fallen weeks ago. Rain, real rain, never came. I thirst for this heavy rain that forms rivulets everywhere. I want to feel on my tongue the large drops that fall. Several people, including Carlos, open their umbrellas. Others take shelter under the trees. I prefer to feel the rain on my body.

Leaving Carmen's grave, Carlos sees me wet, comes over and offers me his umbrella. We walk together to the cemetery exit. Unable to stand the silence between us, Diana takes control to tell Carlos how my month began, with the death of Leo and of another cat that is probably still in the freezer of the woman with Greek features... I immediately regret seeming to compare the death of a cat with human death; to diminish the meaning of Carmen's loss, Carlos' lifelong companion. To correct my gaffe, I commit another:

– I can easily arrange a cat to keep Lia company. In fact, we already have a kitten with four white paws, Josafá, Lia's own son. As you know, incest between cats is not a problem. But there'll never be another Carmen, right? – It's ridiculous to say that and unfair to Leo, also irreplaceable.

Carlos listens attentively, and when he learns that Leo was run over, he gives the impression of adding a little more sorrow to what he already feels.

– One death announced the other – I observe.

It was sudden, in the early morning hours, he relates. Carmen was asleep, at least she didn't suffer, it was an easy death. Then he thanks me for coming. He sends his regards to my "partner," that's the word he uses, referring to Berta.

– He must think we're a couple – I comment to Berta at night in a playful tone.

– That old bird is crazy – she says, wearing the same leopard dress, having already forgotten my criticism. And she changes the subject. – Aninha, I got a great idea from a Lebanese guy. You can buy fake birth certificates in a little town in Goiás. The only problem is the cost: six thousand *reais*.

I end the day improving my theory of the drunken pendulum, which I have been thinking about for months and that goes something like this:

Worlds, clouds of smoke, stains that spread in all directions, leave voids, holes of incoherence. They are kaleidoscopes that change clothes with every changing thought, their parts randomly creating at every moment the forms of their dance. Then everything alters constantly in an absolute indeterminism. The splendor of chaos that Chicão talked about belongs to the deep nature of world order.

I have to know how, in the midst of these shapeless smoke clouds, to look for some direction, a place to rest my eyes. This place is the instant. It is of little importance that the ports of arrival are transitory. That there are no definite answers. That conclusions are also provisional. I am not going to stay frozen like a statue, when in every port I can be carried by new winds of reality.

In every spot on the horizon, in every instant, there is a pendulum inebriated by the ebb and flow of the tides. It moves to and fro propelled by external questions. It follows its own unknown drunken journey that never retraces its path, advancing here, retreating there, moving over there, always swaying from one side to the other.

It's hard to make the transition from the larger meaning of this pendulum's tottering journey to the minute and concrete meaning of my own existence. I understand that the sands of my daily life are dragged by the tides' ebb and flow and participate in the ritual of the ocean.

Perhaps it's my delirium. I look through the shapeless cloud of smoke. I try to see if I can find a port of arrival. There in the distance, I see a question mark called Berta who always goes out at night carrying a gun, and it's my fault. I'm sorry I ever offered her the pistol.

It's late. I see the light on in Carlos' bedroom. I feel sorry for him. It makes me want to go over there again to say that if he needs me, he only has to call; to repay his kindness when he came to my aid after hearing the shots I fired at the burglars.

Not even Diana would dare do something like that, perhaps because tonight even she has no strength. Even so, after considerable hesitation I call Carlos – it's the first time I've ever done this – to tell him that he can count on me if he needs anything. When he answers the phone, I don't have the courage to speak. I hang up. I feel terrible for my foolishness.

It hasn't even been two weeks since Carmen's death when he brings me a present of some begonias planted in a pot. Without worrying about how dark a night it is, he wants to see my garden, where he gives me suggestions on how to care for certain plants and promises to bring me others. He talks about species native to the Plateau, some of the oldest on Earth. Then he calls my attention to a particularly starry sky, showing me the Southern Cross and other constellations.

Around that time Regina arrives, bringing Juliana for surgery. Juliana is very cute. She turns the house upside down. She shares a room with Vera and almost drives her crazy. She also gets in the way of my story writing, interrupting me whether it's to complain about the pain, or to utter the most preposterous questions and observations. I hide my impatience. I want to be her Auntie. I answer every question and comment on every one of her observations.

It was useless to try to make space for two beds in Berta's room; she starts sleeping in the living room. She suggests the arrangement, realizing that sharing a room with Regina is not so easy. Before Regina arrived, she had asked me: "Don't give me away, ok?"

They had never met before. I predicted that in the beginning Berta would be uncomfortable with Regina's neurotic conservative mindset, but would soon get used to it.

– Promise you won't tell her anything about my past as a man? – Berta begs me again.

– I promise – I reassure her.

The antipathy between Regina and Berta is laid bare when Vera announces that she's going to live with Luís.

– I'm not going to marry him. Only live with him – she explains.

At first Berta thinks, as I do, that it's hasty. She tries to intervene, but it's worse. Luís screams that he doesn't owe her anything, and she's in no position to give advice, so don't interfere in his life. This leaves her devastated in a way I have never seen.

Vera also becomes annoyed:

– This is because you all have the wrong concept of marriage.

– I thought you weren't going to marry him – I argue.

– I'm not going to get married *yet* – she emphasizes – but our union is worth more than any of your marriages (yours and your friends') because we love each other. This is forever.

– I'm happy for you. Just don't be cruel, Vera. You don't know what my only marriage was like – I say defending myself.

– You barely know this boy… And you're both too young! – Regina tries to reason.

– At least I won't end up an old maid, like you – Vera retorts rudely.

Alone with Regina, I take Vera's side when I notice a racist basis for my sister's opposition.

– Think what Tereza would do if she were in your place. The boy is from another social class – she puts it that way because she doesn't dare admit that what bothers her is that he's black.

– Vera is an adult now, responsible for her own actions, and what's more: what happens is beyond our control – I try to make her see.

Berta undoubtedly overhears our conversation, because she changes her mind, taking her son's defense, despite the insults she was forced to swallow. She even yells at Regina that he's good enough for my niece, and that we shouldn't interfere in their decision.

After she threatens to move out of the house, Vera finally tells me the reason for the hasty marriage: she's pregnant. She hasn't decided yet whether she should simply have an abortion. She doesn't want to raise a child alone. But Luís is prepared to acknowledge paternity and live with her.

That's when everything hits the fan. These are days of tears and arguments, until I go with Vera to a clinic. She doesn't suffer much physically. She goes home right afterward and needs only one day of rest. But I notice how depressed she is. By some miracle we manage to do everything discreetly, without Berta's knowledge. She's sure that the marriage didn't happen mainly because of Regina's objections.

Not even two months after Carmen's death, Carlos calls me with an invitation to go to the movies.

– May I take Regina? You'll like her – I suggest, convinced that socially she always functions well.

He invites us for tea in the late afternoon. From there we'll leave for the movie. *Tristana* is showing in a Buñuel festival. I'm curious to see this film again to confirm the image that I kept of it and which is mixed up with that phase of my life when I felt like a cold and distant Catherine Deneuve, asphyxiated by that jealous man protecting me, bringing me flowers, presents, fawning over me, begging me not to leave him, saying he loved me, wanting me to love him, to want him.

We don't fall in love either by obligation or by choice. Desire wanders aimlessly. Passionate love can't be requested or won. We love by chance. So I couldn't force love, or even desire, much less passion to be rekindled. That way it wouldn't be love, desire, or passion, it would only be pretense. There was nothing I could do to make the attraction that I once had for Eduardo return. It was useless for him to cry, to beg that we make an effort to reconnect, to become depressed. This only increased my distance from him.

We leave Juliana, now in a cast, with Berenice and go, Regina taking as a gift one of the bottles of *cachaça* that she brought from Taimbé, according to her as good as the Salinas *cachaça*. Before we go in, she asks me:

– This widower is rich, is he?

– I don't know if he's rich. I feel very sorry for him. He's all alone.

It's the second time I visit Carlos' house – we only run into each other on the sidewalk – and the first time I was so nervous... I notice his pipe on the table, the antique clock on the wall, the heavy dark furniture, the velvet-covered chairs so inappropriate for Brasília's heat. There's also a guitar in one corner.

Carlos doesn't hide his interest in Regina. She always was more outgoing and practical than I was. When we were teenagers, she turned all of my platonic lovers into her boyfriends. A single smile from her attracted the attention that my shyness deflected. I don't say that the situation is repeating itself, only because I don't feel anything but affection for Carlos, nothing more.

The tea encourages conversation. Since we missed the time for the movie showing, Carlos decides to make spaghetti. It's eleven at night when we return home, with the certainty that something is going to happen between Regina and Carlos.

The delirious progression of their relationship is explained by the pragmatism of them both. Within a few weeks they're making wedding plans. I'm happy for Regina. She'll dispel the illusion that she has missed something basic in life. She always thought that my parents favored me. I had left for a good life, while she stayed behind, sacrificing herself, taking care of the house, our parents, and Tereza on her deathbed. I, the shy one, had married. She, the outgoing one, had remained an old maid.

To celebrate their engagement, we decided to have a get-together at the house, with the presence of Marcelo, Chicão, Berta, her son Luís, Vera, Formiga… Joana, too, who passing through Brasília, is the first to arrive; she comes in without knocking, calling my name, happy, saying that she's glad to see me again after so long. I can barely hide that I'm not the slightest bit happy to see her. She's still the same. In quick succession she makes several complaints: about her help, the way she was treated by the taxi driver, the way some women are, the behavior of husbands, the difficult life she has. I can't control myself:

– You don't realize that you have a very comfortable easy life.

– How do you know? – she asks, without losing her attitude, and adds:

– Alaíde and Eduardo send regards. They would have liked to come spend New Year's with you. And Cadu, it goes without saying, is thrilled to pieces by the idea of the reunion.

We talk about the ceremony that we plan to have at the cemetery during our end of year gathering.

– What a morbid idea! – Joana opines.

– I only suggested honoring her. It was Maria Antônia who suggested the cemetery – I explain.

– We should have a mass said – Berta says.

– And receive holy Prozac – Chicão adds.

– Since when did you become a Catholic? – I ask Berta, surprised by her suggestion.

– I didn't believe in God, you know? But one day, I decided to ask Him for something. That He show me who I really was. There was no doubt: He whispered that I was homosexual – she says.

Regina rolls her eyes.

– What's a homosexual? – Juliana asks.

– I mean, homosexual was later, back then I was a queer, a queen, Juliana. And ever since, I've been a Christian – Berta says.

– A queen? – Juliana asks.

Carlos gives a chuckle, which irritates Regina even more. With his back to us on the sofa, Luís is visibly uncomfortable.

– Heterosexuality and homosexuality are nineteenth-century inventions. The Greeks didn't recognize that distinction – Chicão pontificates.

– I ask myself if I should be a feminist or keep helping the gay movement – Berta says to him.

– In the old days, everyone knew what a man was and what a woman was – Chicão says. He goes on to argue that gay liberation helps male masculinity: – Boys have to keep proving their manhood because of the prejudice against gays. Ask Cadu – he provokes, turning to Joana.

– He's a real man – she answers – and I can't complain.

– My problem is I'm homeless, have no handkerchief, no documents, no money, just a lick and a promise. In fact, I have a lick with no promise. If there's a club of people like that, I'll join – Berta says. She pauses and concludes, still speaking to Chicão – I'm a real woman, you know? I even wanted to have another child, to revel in maternity. To adopt a baby, like you two.

Carlos looks like a fish out of water. He follows the conversation with smiles and eyebrow movements; silently, just like Regina at his side. Seeing the two of them, I feel as if she were stealing Carlos from me. It's all my fault. Even at my age I'm still shy, not even Diana can help me. My consolation is that Carlos is not really for me. I would never take a relationship with him seriously.

– I've already made all the arrangements, you know. I'm going to be Mona Habib for six thousand *reais* – Berta tells me with a shaky voice and a glass of *caipirinha* in her hand. – Mona Habib is an invented name, but there is a real Lebanese couple who are going to appear as my parents on the document. The danger is that one day I'll run into them, can you imagine? Or they'll go to the records office to request the birth certificates of all their children and discover they have an extra daughter. The forger swore that the whole family returned to Lebanon. I just don't have the six thousand *reais* yet, right? Look, Aninha, I need documents as a woman. Because we change sex, but if we're still a man on the ID card, it's no good. I want to be a woman on paper. *On paper!* The police stop me, and when they see I'm a man they treat me worse than a whore. Mona... I like the name. It's the perfect name, don't you think? Mona... I have to get used to the new name. Let's see: Mona Habib will wear glasses, dye *all – aaalll* – her hair blonde, wear blue contact lenses, and draw a mole on her face. What do you think?

I prefer not to comment.

Then she blows me away with this pearl:

– The name is more important than the pussy, I can even do without that. In an emergency, we can always offer ass.

I am shocked by the joke that Regina also hears. Then Berta is roaring with Joana. When I draw near she murmurs:

– For her I'd be a man, a man like I never was. I'm sorry I ever had the surgery.

– Enough of this nonsense – Chicão says.

I make a film in my head of the two women, thinking about the day that on Joana's suggestions we – she, a friend of hers and I –

went to the sauna at the National Hotel. I'll never forget the grotesque scene of several naked women sweating buckets, arguing, Joana talking loudly. Her big breasts, American Playboy style, had inverted nipples. But, without a doubt, she had a beautiful body. Her friend was very thin, tall and buck-toothed, with almost no breasts. She invited us later for drinks at her apartment, and when she left, Joana made a strange comment that she and I had something profound in common, an incontrovertible connection. I ignored her, but from then on I felt genuine repugnance for her.

After the guests leave, I stay talking to Regina until late. I decide to explain what she already knows full well. I don't feel any obligation to keep my promise to Berta not to reveal her open secret, since she was already so indiscreet herself.

Regina then tells me that Carlos had deduced from a comment Berta made that she and I were a couple, and when Regina showed shock at that assumption, he amended, as if it helped, that he was in favor of gay marriage.

– What a bitch! – I say, furious.

– You're going to have to decide between that transvestite and me. It's not prejudice, but if she stays here I'm not staying another day.

I know that Regina is a cheapskate and won't want to pay for a hotel. But I agree with her. And it's not only because of what she tells me that my patience with Berta is running out.

In the same conversation, Regina announces with no emotion that her engagement to Carlos has no future. She doesn't love him. I give her pragmatic advice that I would never take, containing some of the bitterness provoked by my life with Eduardo:

– Marrying for love is a mistake, Regina. You can be sure it won't last, because the courting and desire soon end. Only forbidden love lasts.

– There you go with your theories.

The next day I fire off my anger against Berta:

– You're nuts, you know? Saying those things in front of your son… You need a good analysis.

– I don't believe in those things. What do I have to do with some story that Freud had the hots for his mother and was afraid of incest?

I lay my cards on the table:

– It bothers me that you go out at night so often. In this era of AIDS, it's important to be careful.

– If you're trying to insinuate, I am not a prostitute, ok? – She looks at me with her head up, puffs up her chest, and puts her hands on her hips.

She didn't have to say it in so many words, I am worried about precisely that. The heavy make-up, fake eyelashes, bright red polish on the long nails, the frequent perfect leg waxings, the black hose and garters, the gold belts and mile-high heels, short skirts, all of this, together, signal the care of a professional. But I deny it:

– No, it never occurred to me that you were selling yourself. What I'm worried about is promiscuity in this era of AIDS.

– You're prejudiced against people like me. You don't believe that I'm only interested in finding someone who loves me. You think I've been with different men right and left.

– Pardon me, but you used to have that reputation.

– That was a long time ago; I'm a different person.

Controlling my temper I go right to the point:

– So you told Carlos that we're a lesbian couple?

Surprised, Berta gives a nervous laugh.

– That's a good one! Even when Carmen was alive, that old busybody was always making a pass at me. Just because I decided to tell him to kiss off, he invented that story. Never would I ever insinuate something like that! Yes, once I said that you and I were friends for life, right? And that's true, we are friends for life, right? I may indeed have repeated what you yourself told me: that we make a perfect couple, better than if we were married…

– Look, living together is becoming very difficult.

– Calm down. I was just about to tell you that I'm leaving. I've already taken too much advantage of your hospitality and patience. But as friends, ok? I only have reasons to thank you for everything you've done for me.

She starts to cry, she's a poor devil, yes she's the one who's alone in the world, no family, no one, her family wants nothing to do with her, it's as if she didn't have parents or siblings. I'm the only real friend she has ever found.

I know that her suffering is real. Even though my Ana side with the soft heart wants to sympathize, Diana doesn't allow her emotions to confuse her, she wants to throw Berta out of the house. And she's right to maintain her coldness, because it's becoming too much of a burden to feed Berta on my shrinking salary. Diana and Ana continue to struggle over what to say:

– You can stay here until you find a place to live.

– No. I prefer to leave right now – she says proudly.

– Don't be crazy.

– It's better this way. I'll manage; I have somewhere to go. Later I'll be in touch.

So I let Berta leave, under the indifference of Berenice, Vera, and Formiga.

When I tell Chicão that I suspect she went to Joana's hotel, she comments:

– Joana is an exact Capitu monkey.

She's not referring to the Machado de Assis heroine, who possibly betrayed her husband with his best friend, but to the monkey in the Brasília zoo, who learned to swim so that she could escape her island to have sex with a monkey from another species on the other bank, under the desperate watch of her husband, on this side.

– Berta took only one small suitcase with part of her wardrobe. She'll be back before long, at least to get her things. It only frightened me not to find the gun above the wardrobe – I tell Chicão.

– She may never return – he throws his raw realism in my face.

– I already miss her – I say.

– You have a guilty conscience – he answers. – You're paying the price for your moralizing and prejudice.

– Me? Prejudiced?

– You're a bitch! Of course it was your fucking fault.

– And nothing up the ass?

– Everything, my dear. Everything – he says liltingly, rolling his eyes, limp-wristed.

A few days after Berta's departure, Rui calls to thank me for the card I sent on his birthday. We have a quick conversation. "Write, and if you come through Brasília look me up," I tell him.

I could have said more, however I'm not anxious to see him again, and I doubt if it's worthwhile to approach him in such a cold manner, as if my age conceded to the sacrifice of bearing his ugliness. But I hope that he doesn't give up and stays in touch.

It's November. My loneliness increases with the return of Juliana and Regina to Minas and, from the large living room window, nature has suddenly become green.

4

SUICIDAL PASSIONS

All of the Useless, with the exception of Berta, contact me before our reunion. It's a hot summer day, Monday, December 27, when Cadu telephones that he wants to see me. Why did he tell me he's alone? Why this enthusiasm? This friendliness? He never wasted time in his mission to seduce. He spared neither Helena, nor obviously Eva nor Joana. I always escaped his overtures. I don't think he ever found me attractive.

Cadu's sensuality is not selfish or narcissistic; it's generous. He would be capable of sacrificing his own life for a woman's body. He is a hero of a vain heroism. An idealist of an illusory ideal. His illusion is to think it possible to fill life solely with sex, repeating the attempt with every woman. This isn't living in a void, as many people believe. It's filling the void with enthusiasm and pleasure – momentary, of course. What enthusiasm and pleasure are not momentary?

He sees the world as freedom and hope. His ideal causes less damage and is more within reach than many other equally illusory ideals – national, ethnic, religious, political – that have mobilized men's actions so stupidly... There is a certain freshness – a white kernel of innocence – in his attitude. An endless youth... A joy... A desire to please the women he falls in love with, truly falls in love with. He is certainly capable of loving one woman while pursuing others for his passing pleasures.

Chicão disagrees with everything I think about Cadu. And the disdain that Japona has for him hides a trace of resentment. Besides provoking envy, Cadu is a threat to other men, fearful of seeing their women succumb to his charms. It seems unacceptable that a man can be so loved by women, despite not devoting himself exclusively to any one of them, solely because of his unequalled physical beauty and lecherous smile, irresistible appeal and blind confidence in life. No, I'm not convinced that Cadu is ridiculous, as Chicão says, although I imagine that he'll be ridiculous one day if, with age, he doesn't change his behavior.

This opinion of mine was also never shared by the women in our group. Neither Maria Antônia nor Helena, much less any of the university colleagues who met Cadu, ever dared to defend him, perhaps because that would make them cheap. It would be the equivalent of revealing a secret; that they could feel pleasure in an uncommitted sexual relationship, which they knew beforehand would go nowhere. Nevertheless, they made a point of saying that he had propositioned them and they had refused. In my opinion, Maria Antônia capitulated and kept quiet about it.

I never heard say that he went around bragging about his activities, despite the revelation that Maria Antônia made one day about the size of his penis. He told her that it measured nineteen centimeters erect. We laughed at the story, Maria Antônia, Helena, and I. We didn't have any point of reference; on a ruler later we saw exactly what that corresponded to and we thought it a bit extraordinary.

When Cadu calls me, I immediately remember that yellowed page that I couldn't destroy and that describes my dream about him, me at a party at Joana's house – which in the dream is an enormous house with a garden overlooking the ocean – me on the verandah, like the verandah on a Minas plantation house, where hammocks sway in the wind.

It must be because of memories and neediness hardened by years of sexual abstinence that now on the telephone I don't just like the fact that Cadu is interested in me, but also fantasize my own isle of love. After we make a date and he hangs up, I revel in reading that page yellowed by time that I didn't have the courage to throw away. There my dream with him is narrated in all its details, me on the verandah, waving to the people scattered around the garden; then I recline on the railing looking at the movement of the guests. Suddenly Cadu comes up behind me and touches my waist, descends along my belly, runs over my legs, my genitals, and kisses my shoulders and fondles my breasts. I feel chills on my neck while I look at the incandescent red of the geraniums on the balcony. He lifts my dress (I think it's black muslin…) and I feel that hard thing rubbing behind me. I look at the people down below in the garden, they continue to talk, some are looking at me. And we pretend it's nothing; I bend one leg on the railing and feel him entering me, as in extremely slow motion. The people in the garden become embarrassed. A mixture of sharp pain, dizziness, I shudder. Still faster. And suddenly he tries to put it in my ass, and then I don't like it, and I say out loud: "Not that way." Eduardo wakes me and asks what's the matter. I wake up wet.

That page reminds me how alive my sexuality was at the start of our marriage and that's also why I didn't want to destroy it, just as for other reasons I didn't want to get rid of Rui's letter. Eduardo liked anal sex. I let him, he had to go very slowly, it hurt, and over time I lost the pleasure and felt only the pain, until I got the impression that for him I was nothing more than an ass. He didn't look at me, and if he looked, he didn't see me. He hardly ever said a word to me, he only wanted to fuck.

I had begun to think I would be able to throw that page with the dream about Cadu in the trash if, in my story, I made a list of the men in my life, who weren't that many and, with the exception of Eduardo, added little to it. With the first guy I felt no pleasure at all, but I thought it was cool to be in a motel losing my virginity at seventeen. I didn't know for sure what a hard dick was; I looked at his and I wasn't sure what it really meant. After that, there was a little of everything, from my lust for Paulinho to my rejections of Rui. Perhaps the most daring was when Diana fucked in the hall with a classmate's boyfriend.

But neither was I able to write about the men in my life, nor throw out that sheet of paper.

My latent desire for Cadu began in that dream. Now that he phones, it occurs to me that since I wasn't able to throw the paper away, I need to throw Cadu himself in the trash after using him. After using him without limits, without fear or remorse.

I didn't know that in my twenties I'd had a crush on him – or I didn't want to know. He dated Eva, flirted with Joana, and I couldn't accept having any intimacy with him. I liked for him to hug me, to hold my hands, they were his idiosyncrasies, and I felt my spirit warm when I saw him… Photography brought us together. Always with that kind of sentimental distance that we called respect, he took photographs of me that he called sensual, he touched me lightly, raising my dress above the knee so that "just a bit" of my "sculptural thighs" – his words – would show; he praised my lips and gave me a look that provoked a shudder in my soul and was stuck in the back of my mind for days. I liked it when he kissed – really kissed – my face. Sometimes, when we greeted each other, our puckered lips touched. There was nothing special in this; that was the way he greeted almost all women. Our lips lit a spark of emotion that sent a tingling throughout my body. One day he invited me to lunch, and at some point we held hands and a sweet energy from our hands made me quiver inside.

Now, preparing to see him, Diana even buys black see-through lingerie and thong panties. At the last moment, I doubt my body's virtues and the old question returns: "What will he think?" Diana tells me it doesn't matter. While she and I argue, I look for items more appropriate to the occasion among my underwear. I put on white lace panties. I try on a short tight dress that shows off my body. I'm no longer twenty, I'm more attractive if I cover up more. I have a black leather skirt… A corset, garters and hose… I check myself in the mirror, from the front, the back… I'll go like this. I put on a silk blouse and my gold earrings and ring braided in an art deco design.

– I may be home late. And if I don't come home, don't worry – I tell Berenice.

After dinner, Cadu drives me home. There was none of the expected chemical reaction between us. When it's obvious that nothing's going to happen, I force the issue out of pure desire to follow my plan.

– Don't you want to come in? – I ask.

So that they don't feel less manly, I know that men like him find themselves obligated by a woman's invitation, almost any woman's. I recall Berta's phrase: "All women are easy or hard, depending on the situation and for whom. Men, however, are always easy."

My tactic works. The cards are all on the table. Cadu suggests taking me to the apartment at the beginning of the North Wing, where he is alone, the friend who lent it to him is out of town.

– I always had the hots for you. But I thought I'd take it on the chin because you never gave me the time of day – he says, when we get there.

– I was shyer than I am now, if that's possible. But you're right. I would have been incapable of having an affair with a lady's man like you.

He doesn't give me a chance to regret my comment, which he seems not even to hear. While he hugs and kisses me and runs his hands under my skirt, he rationalizes:

– What we're doing isn't against anyone. It's not against Joana. It's just for us. We have everything to gain and nothing to lose.

He didn't notice my skirt, or my blouse, or my earrings, or my ring. He delights in my corset, unfastens my garters, and praises my panties while removing them. He insists on refastening my hose and garters and asks me to turn around, he wants to see me from all sides. I suggest hiding my body in the shadows. Cadu wants light, he says that age has filled out my thighs and my rump, he likes them this way, they're softer.

– You were always beautiful, but too thin. Now you're better than ever – words that are like music, although the notes ring false. – I love your brown skin. The mixture of all the world's races will produce a brown like this – he says, when I stretch out on the bed.

Diana wants to look like a vulgar woman, to give herself with no shame. Everything or nothing. Or better yet everything. I fear what could happen, but in fact, I let everything happen.

He puts on a condom mechanically. Standing over the floor, he drags me to the edge of the bed. He lifts my legs into the air spread-eagled, hooking them over his shoulders, and I hang there, like a ham.

– I'm dying to fuck you – he says.

– Slowly. Very slowly – I repeat.

He doesn't hear, he goes too fast and it burns, even hurts, but I don't say anything. I can't get wet, I'm tense and nervous with this annoying pain, the walls of my vagina burning with his movements; I see him as a dog, faster and faster on top of me, and then he trembles in orgasm, he lies that he never felt such pleasure, "wow, what a great fuck." I'm still apprehensive. "Was it good for you?" he asks, and I say yes. His body, now relaxed on the bed, satiated and submerged in the emptiness that comes after orgasm, has already lost its former elegance.

– Do you think fidelity is important? – he inquires, still lying on the bed, looking at the ceiling.

– Yes, but love is more important. What desire and passion decide may be wrong; but what love decides is always right – I answer, lying next to him, still wearing the corset and noticing that my hose are shredded on the insides of my thighs.

– The worst catastrophe for a man is betrayal by a woman.

It's dangerous to ask if he's referring to Joana. It must have been hard for Eduardo to discover that there was someone else in my life, to know that I couldn't love him. Perhaps I wasn't in love with Paulinho; perhaps he was an accessory to my love. Perhaps he was only the obvious circumstantial cause of my lust, an egoistic lust that fed on my own sentimental problems. I can't be who I'm not, my goodness was mixed with the coldness of an assassin of Eduardo's soul. It's as if I were seeing his disappointed face now. "I feel like shit, crawling at your feet," he told me in a pathetic tone, and I didn't know how to answer. In his attacks of jealousy he used violence to try to keep me at home. The beginning of the end – that I never told anyone and that I didn't settle with the police only out of cowardice – was when he made me have sex, I tried to bite him with all the strength in my teeth; he's much stronger than I am, it's better to say exactly what in fact happened, that he tore my underwear, pried open my legs, he tried to force himself on me; we were home alone and it did no good for me to yell, no one heard me, "you whore!" he screamed, while he was trying to get inside me, I struggled as much as I could; he was only able to insert a finger that tore me, and he rubbed against me and came on my stomach and hurt me; I had bruises all over my thighs, my whole body – it was a rape, I can't call it anything else. When I had that nervous breakdown and decided to leave after Paulinho's disappearance, he reacted by retreating, going silent and insisting that I come back. But I couldn't erase what had happened, like some machine, which only added to a past of hurt and resentment.

I look at Cadu and say:

– Infidelity is hard to face, but it's possible to overcome if there is love. I left Eduardo because I thought that he didn't love me. Today I think that marriage and love are truly incompatible.

We fell asleep together.

– I like women who don't get attached, don't fall in love. Who know how to see sex as a game – he tells me in the morning.

– I'm not like that – I try to dot the i's.

He laughs; perhaps he thinks I'm not serious.

– Do you like mangoes? – he wants to know.

– I love them.

He goes down to the mango trees facing the Avenue. I look out the blinds. To the south, a perfectly clear sky over a sun-drenched landscape. To the north, from the sky to the ground I clearly see the line of rain that's advancing and an enormous 180° rainbow, like the one that framed the middle of the Plateau thirty years ago, when Iris made prophecies and under a heavy rain Cadu helped me fill a little jar with soil. The boys are playing soccer. A river of cars races toward the Esplanade of Ministries. I look at the rows of mango trees. Among them, Cadu, like a child, jumps to pick bunches of mangoes for me.

I revert to my childhood pulping the mangoes that Cadu brings me, sucking them from the stem end and smearing myself all over with juice. We bathe together in the tub, and then he uses a dryer on my hair and carries me in his arms to the divan. We stay here talking while he caresses me under the towel in which I'm wrapped, and when he uncovers me, I strike the pose of an Ingres odalisque. He asks me to lie over the rounded edge of the divan. I'm offered up, the curves of my buttocks following those of the divan, and I feel his dick caress my thighs and slide between them until it kisses the lips of my stunned vulva. He embraces me from behind, penetrates me, almost ceremoniously, and whispers in my ear:

– I'm in love with you. You are the most exciting woman in the world, did you know that?

I hear an enormous crash and the weather darkens, I see the heavy rain that starts to run down the windows, and while he's penetrating me I become more excited, feeling pleasure, only pleasure.

– Do you want me to stick it all in? – he asks.

And shameless Diana answers with pleasure:

– Fuck me, fuck me crazy. I'm dying to fuck you!

In thick honey my pleasure envelops his hard dick, a dancing dagger of hard steel that rises between my cheeks, presses my valley, explores my other hole, wallows in my deepest place. My knees touch the floor as if I were praying to Bacchus and were offering myself as sacrifice, a flash of lightning projects our shadows on the walls, the clap of thunder trembles inside me and it becomes dark again and I want him to hurt me and he hurts me and I command:

– Say that I'm your little whore.

– And he insults me with affection, calling me "my little whore" and worse things, and his hands squeeze my breasts, as if they wanted to remove all the milk that isn't there, and his dagger plunges into my deepest pain, and with its famished head extracts another deeper orgasm, when I fall vertiginously over the well of corruption where I bathe in spring water.

Once again seated on the divan, my eyes must wear some look of sadness from weariness and contentment.

– Stop, stay just where you are. Keep your face in that position, the light is perfect – Cadu orders me.

I recline on the divan, semi-wrapped in a sheet that leaves most of my body exposed.

– What gorgeous curves! – he exclaims. – I want to take your picture. Your face won't show, just part of your body.

– No, please. I would never be comfortable with that.

Light filtered by the rain leaves shadows in the room. I notice something serious and sober in the features of Cadu's partially darkened face. I see everything in black and white, contrasts of light and gray. And then we lie on the bed, listening to the noise of the rain and watching the dance of shadows on the ceiling.

He kisses me slowly all over my body. With his tongue he excites me between my legs. He caresses my lips with his penis that grows and fills my mouth; I suck eagerly until his semen spills onto my face, and then he doesn't want to stop, he rests his exhausted body on top of mine and we still make love, with him on top rubbing his belly against mine.

– There's nothing in this world better than fucking you. I want to fuck you like this, non-stop, my whole life. I can't believe you opened your legs for me, you're doing me... Tell me you like doing me.

– I love doing you.

– It's not like fucking an inexperienced young girl, it's like eating ripe fruit; I like breasts like these – he touches me lightly – thighs like these, a belly like this – he runs his hands – an ass like this, fleshy, that's a pleasure to grab – he plants his hands under me – pubes like this... – He goes in and out a little at a time, in and out, first slowly and then faster, like in the dream I had about him; with his eyes staring at my open thighs, fucking me with his eyes too, in and out, in and out, in and out, harder and faster.

I even begin to believe that he really likes me when he comes again, this time with screams and loud moans; he can't come that many times if he doesn't like me. I remember his nickname and Diana says "you do have the world's sweetest dick," I am powerful because desire is power, the very power to desire, to want to live, he makes high voltage electricity spill from my entrails, at the source of my orgasm, and I join his cries and moans, and I don't care whether the neighbors hear, I want no limits on this excess.

Without past or future, I learn: this is the instant, real time full of events, that don't run or flee, don't advance or retreat, just are. This time that doesn't last is not time, it doesn't end or exist forever. It neither goes by nor do I go by it, and therefore I just am; and yet I am a stray bullet that shatters on impact. Cadu caresses me. I try to tell him, in the simplest terms I can, that this moment with him enlightens me on the meaning of instantaneity. Without understanding, he answers me, our bodies still entwined:

– It's like the arrow of the Zen archer, released at the instant that the eye focuses on the target with perfect precision. Like in photography.

I spend my time over the next few days meditating and rummaging through old papers. I feel numb. I am also hurt, physically and spiritually. I spend hours between my room and the bathroom, between the bed and the dressing table mirror... I'm almost unable to sit on the bidet where I wash at length, distracted, massaging myself while a sharp pain rises inside me.

Behind the picture Norberto did of me, I glue the sheet of paper that I still can't destroy – the one of the dream about Cadu. A man like that, who thinks I'm beautiful and is tender, is enough for me. It's not possible for Cadu always to perform this well, for me to be just one more woman in his life. This can't have been just another one-night stand, with me Cadu felt much more than momentary passion. I keep imagining how I'll be able to face him and Joana when they arrive for the reunion of the Useless. I didn't invite her. He told me that she's coming, so that she doesn't spend the millennium New Year's Eve alone.

Poisoned by Cupid's arrow, I lock myself in my room. It never occurred to me that at fifty-five I would want to be more mature, to satisfy myself completely with a man. Life is a never-ending search, always finished midway through. Nature – God, for those who believe – didn't plan humanity well. Or is it the fault of the human species that didn't know how to evolve? Can all these pages, here to the left of my bed, still teach me something about love?

I am in love like a teenager. Cadu, like Paulinho before, has nothing to do with this. The reason for this emotional whirlwind is inside me, just as it was during that earlier event. Cadu simply helped me to burst a dam inside me, where the violent waters of passion race uncontrolled and wild, headed I know not where. I am alone in this boat of passion. Cadu spent just one night with me, like he would spend with any other easy woman who offered herself like a whore. He doesn't even think about me any more. I put myself in Eva's skin and I understand her better than ever. For such a great unrequited passion, only suicide.

Anxious, I call Cadu. Joana answers, and I speak to her with the impression that my voice sounds phony and that I'm revealing my secrets.

– Any news from Berta? – I ask.

– None. The only time I saw her was at your house.

I hope that Berta shows up at the reunion of the Useless.

The day before the reunion, Chicão comes by so we can select a reading from the Philosopher's book. I remember that little jar of soil, the one that Cadu helped me fill. I set it on the table, so that it's very visible. It comes from the mystic journey that we made – all nine of us – to the Garden of Salvation. A journey in more than one sense. We went in two cars driving north, under the effects of pot, and listening to funeral music on the radio. The twisted, still-green trees went by rapidly on both sides of the road. In the sky, opening like a fan, a starburst of colored rays.

When we crossed under the neon arch of the Garden of Salvation someone informed us that the priestess was inviting us to a ceremony at the Altered Waters. We put on white gowns over our clothes and took one of three full buses. Almost all of the passengers were residents of the Garden of Salvation, we noticed by the golden accessories, the hats and the talk about cosmic revelations.

We came to an open field and disembarked. We went up a trail cutting through the thorny brush. Atop the hill, surrounding Iris, a circle of people. She wore her long flowing white robes, striped with blue ribbons.

– On this fifteenth parallel there was a ceremonial center for the people of the ancient kitchen middens, the first inhabitants of Brazil, before the Jês and the Tupis. – she expounds – Through this area passed the Tapuias, Xavantes and Timbiras. Even today there are Avá-Canoeiros in Minaçu-Cavalcante; Tapuias in Nova América Rubiataba; Kaypós to the south; Xavantes in Pem Pium; Bororos to the west; and Timbiras on the northern plateaus. This is the site for us to prepare for the third millennium. To imbue ourselves with the spirit of the next humanity. The Central Plateau is the oldest part of the Americas. It's also where there is the best chance of surviving the cataclysms that are predicted.

Then a one hundred and eighty degree rainbow appeared in the sky.

– This is the witchcraft of our Greco-mound Goddess – Chicão says, with a touch of irony.

We should look at the sky. There she was, the goddess of the rainbow, the messenger of the gods cited in the *Iliad*.

I was never mystical. But Chicão's coldness didn't infect me. The atmosphere enveloped me. The rainbow that appeared by chance added mystery and beauty to the ceremony, in which the vocabulary of Asian and African sects mixed with that of Christianity. Later, I identified a Taoist text that was almost identical to Iris' teachings:

"The great way is calm and the spirit large. Nothing is easy, nothing is difficult. Obey the nature of things." She said this opening her arms in slow motion, while the flowing sleeves of her robe swayed in the wind.

With the rains, the mushrooms had grown on the cow dung. Several people started collecting them and offering them to our group, as if in a communion ceremony. So, we ate them, certain that something magical was going to transpire.

And, in fact, something did. Iris, still as a statue, her hands together pointing up at the sky, eyes closed, started to sweat, she seemed to be feeling a sharp pain. Then, she let out a roar and announced that she was foreseeing the end of the world. Next she distributed little bottles to be thrown into the three rivers, one in each basin.

A cold, heavy, non-stop rain began to fall. We all embraced.

– This water will render us unconscious – Chicão said.

– Let's concentrate on the energy that's passing from one person to another here – Eva requested.

Whatever it was, energy or not, it increased in intensity with every flash of lightning that we saw, every clap of thunder that we heard, and with the rivers of water that rolled down our faces. We laughed and cried at the same time. Ever since, whenever I think of the possibility of human communion, of a single collective feeling, of a shared and unfettered love that demands nothing in return, I recall that moment of reconciliation and profound humanity, when despair and hope were fused.

Right there, holding each other, seeing the water flowing around our feet, we made the reunion pact for New Year's Eve 2000. Eva was the one who proposed it. We should prepare for the next millennium and each of us bring to that gathering an accounting of our lives. I was chosen as the contact person. Everyone should contact me a year before, in 1999. I should then propose a place for the reunion. Our hands were entwined above the mud, and without saying anything Cadu helped me to put some of that mud into the little jar I was still carrying, instead of having thrown it in one of the rivers.

Thirty years later, the bottle is here, ready to witness the return of the Useless. The occasion demands new clothes. I opt for a long black dress, slit up one side to the middle of my thigh, with a plunging back and a subtle front neckline, a cut that discreetly highlights the lines of my body. I buy everything else in black, to match: panties and bra, fishnets, narrow-toed shoes with spike heels. I go to the hairdresser. I call the manicurist to come over. I wax my legs. I take a long bath, one of those that washes my thoughts. I apply foundation carefully to my face, study the eye-shadows in their smallest details, put just a touch of rouge on each cheek, highlight my lashes with mascara, pencil my eyebrows and douse myself in perfume. The rings and earrings are the same ones that I wore to meet Cadu.

It's Friday, December 31, 1999. I select CDs of the Beatles and Caetano. "Transcendental Cinema" is playing when Maria Antônia arrives, around 8:30 pm. After her, others start arriving, Chicão and Marcelo, bringing Marquinhos; Japona and Cássia; and Cadu unaccompanied.

They all retain something of their youthful features, so much that even if I had not seen them since the days when we used to meet, I would have recognized them.

– Marquinhos here has a promising career in uselessness – Chicão says.

– Don't talk about your son that way, not even in jest – Cássia reacts.

– I'm not proposing membership for Valentino in our club only because he already has a place in captivity. You're the most useless of us all, right, Valentino? – Chicão says, with Rodolfo at his side, paying no attention to Cássia.

Rodolfo wags his tail as if he understood.

– Joana sends her regrets. She couldn't resist the fireworks; she stayed in Rio. At the last minute, she accepted an invitation to a party aboard a *bateau mouche* – Cadu explains.

It occurs to me that there might have been a quarrel between him and Joana on my account.

Berta, who demanded that this reunion be held, doesn't even send word. She doesn't want to face being seen by old friends, or else, like Joana, she doesn't want to trade a good New Year's Eve celebration for a dinner with the Useless. I remember her suggestion about the club. No, it must be something else; I understand Berta: there's no reason for her to come, after what happened between us.

Chicão sits in the main armchair, with Rodolfo always at his feet, Marquinhos on his lap.

On the coffee table, the Chinese figurine that Berta gave me observes us through bulging eyes. I am overcome by a strange sensation, as if I were in imminent danger.

I open the first bottle of champagne, one of many they all brought. I don't want to get drunk, but I'm disposed to half a binge that will loosen my tongue without affecting my clarity.

– The idea was for us to meet today to make an accounting – I say.

– It's already done. We're all living in shit – Chicão summarizes.

– I'm not – Maria Antônia refutes.

– The conclusion that we can reach today is the following: we were truly lunatics, right, Valentino? – Chicão says, turning to Rodolfo, lying at his feet.

– Harmless lunatics – I correct. I insist again that thirty years ago we had the idea of meeting on this date to take stock of our lives.

– You were idiots to be taken in by that crazy woman – Chicão says, referring to Iris.

– You're the idiot who compared her to a Greek God – replies Maria Antônia.

– I didn't know her Egyptian side yet – he ironizes, without cracking a smile – a combination of Osiris and Isis. She could only rule the dead.

While he's talking, Josafá sits on the edge of the coffee table, showing his white paws and observing us, as if he were a real Egyptian statue. Lia is with us too, jumping from lap to lap, with Marquinhos following her.

It's a relief to realize that Chicão and Maria Antônia have come to an understanding. They needle each other, but at least they're speaking.

We thought the world was going to be very different in thirty years, right, Ana? – Cadu says to me.

Is he trying to imply something about our extraordinary meeting that week? Before I can formulate a sentence, Japona answers for me:

– And it is, it is a different world, only it's completely different from what we imagined.

– Fear is what's marking the end of the millennium – I opine.

– Today's fears are the same as those of a thousand years ago: fear of violence, poverty, disease, and natural disasters, without even mentioning the fear of the end of the world – Chicão declares.

I look at my painting. It still has the original colors and all the wrinkles that Berta painted. I again have the feeling that I have already reached the age that it shows.

– That fear, I don't have. I am more worried about my own end of the world, which will come before long – I say.

– What's this, Ana? Shut your trap! – Marcelo protests.

– Look, try to hang on. A deceased's life is extremely dull, worse than the life of the living. Ghosts today have even lost the right to scare – Chicão finishes.

Cadu looks at me while raising his champagne glass. I feel a pit in my stomach. I resisted for so many years and I finally gave in to Cadu. I did it, ok. I did it because I wanted to. I even took it in the ass, ok, I have to relax. I don't care that I'm in love, alone in this boat, unrequited. That he looks at me as if I were his whore, his little whore.

– Bravo! To our thirty years of friendship! – he cries.

– To our friendship! – they all reply, almost in unison.

Then they join me in another toast, in memory of Eva, Helena and the Philosopher. I light the incense that Berta had bought to honor Eva.

– Ana, you're going to do me a favor and put out that incense – Cadu requests. –It gives me an allergy. And it smells like the past.

– That's what we want, to remember the past – Maria Antônia complains.

– Only to remember. Smelling is too much already. It smells like mildew – Chicão says.

– If Helena came back to life, she would be a revolutionary again. More than ever, the ingredients for revolution are present, the people are impoverished, many don't even have anything to eat – Maria Antônia explains.

– Don't revive her for that, better to leave her in peace – Chicão replies. He shows the Philosopher's book: – Ana, read the selection we chose.

We stop the music. Everyone goes silent. I stand. My reading takes on the solemn air that priests give Biblical passages during mass:

– A flash of exception, human life is a detour from perfection that consists in the filling of possible places along a funeral procession, where it makes and remakes itself. Death is not just a decisive accident, it doesn't transform life into destiny, because each human life has its own death, finds its own meaning. To each, then, a death according to his or her life. No one can be fully realized in life, only in death, which is complete and perfect...

We are all circumspect. Maria Antônia breathes deeply, as if to alleviate a pain. Marquinhos isn't the only one who looks at us surprised. Japona also stares at us as if we came from Mars.

At last, we sit down at the table, but not before Marcelo puts Marquinhos to sleep. With Chicão and Japona, respectively, to my left and right, I sit at one end of the table, Cadu at the other, with Maria Antônia on his right and Cássia on his left, Marcelo in the center between Maria Antônia and Japona.

For the first course, I serve a light endive salad, to balance the game dish that comes next.

– We came here to celebrate the end of the millennium, didn't we, people? To the new millennium! – cries Maria Antônia.

– It's crazy to celebrate! Everything will be the same as it was last year. No one celebrated the year 1000 – Chicão says.

– They must have celebrated it, too – Cássia argues.

– They only started celebrating the end of the century after the seventeenth century. In the year 1000, Europe didn't even have the zero. Maybe the Mayas already knew about it, but it was from India that it came into Arab mathematics – Chicão takes the opportunity to give a class, after his fashion. – You know? "Zero" comes from the Arabic *sifr*, wind, translated into Latin as *zephirum*. It was only brought to Europe in 990 by the monk Gerbert d'Aurillac, later Sylvester II, who was pope in the year 1000. It only became known two centuries later. A number inspired by emptiness and the desert.

– Very appropriate for Brasília – Maria Antônia says.

– Which is good for nothing – Cadu concludes.

– This here is truly a desert of trees and people – Marcelo agrees.

– The civil servants are empty, the politicians are empty, even if Chicão doesn't agree – Maria Antônia continues.

– It seems that we're all in agreement. The zero is essential for the Useless, after all – I try to conclude, thinking about the symbolism of our reunion, about the zero that should be our renewal.

– And what are we celebrating, then? – Japona asks.

– Two thousand years of Christ – Cássia answers.

– But God doesn't think in round numbers – Chicão says.

The main dish is paca meat marinated overnight in red wine, served with fried manioc meal, rice, and collards. I'm afraid it's a little heavy. I'm relieved when Cássia declares, "It's delicious." Her opinion is enough for me. Of all of us, together with Chicão, she's the one who knows the most about cooking.

– Let's go for theobromine, the food of the gods – Chicão announces when it's time for dessert.

Then Berenice brings the chocolate mousse that Chicão made. I open more bottles of champagne.

– To the Mayans and the Dominican Friars! – he raises his cup.

– Why? – Cássia asks.

– It was the Dominicans who took chocolate to Europe in 1544. They accompanied a delegation of Mayans on a visit to the future Spanish king, Felipe II – Chicão explains.

When we return to the sofas to have our espresso, Cadu's gaze penetrates deep into my soul. I am undone; I don't know how to face him. Suddenly, he removes a small tin from his pocket.

– From theobromine to *Cannabis sativa* – I hear Chicão say.

Cadu starts to roll a joint. Everyone follows the movement of his fingers with their eyes. At last, he slides his tongue over the paper: the cigarette is finished. He lights it, takes a deep draw, and passes it. No one takes a single puff. I haven't smoked in ages. I put the cigarette to my lips and pretend to draw, keeping the smoke in my mouth, so that Cadu doesn't feel out of place.

– You're all squares? Shit, times really have changed! – he protests.

– The times, no. Only us. The young around here are still smoking – Chicão explains.

– I just don't want to lose my memory – Maria Antônia explains.

– You only lose your short-term memory – I give this clarification, recalling what I read in an issue of the health magazine that Vera gives me once in a while.

– You can make up for the destroyed neurons by eating fish heads and chocolate. Chocolate is the big drug – Chicão says.

– Over time I discovered that pot makes me paranoid. I began to value clarity more, the ideas that come to me the hard way. In the end, it's more satisfying to think lucidly – Maria Antônia continues to explain.

There is a moment of silence while everyone observes Cadu's puffs. He smiles at me and says:

– I think that you're the only one, Ana, who's going to keep me company in this cigarette.

We open more bottles of champagne. We hear the fireworks exploding. It's midnight, the start of the New Year, the New Century, the New Millennium.

– Hey, what a thrill! – Marcelo exclaims, waking from a nap.

I call Berenice to join the group, I give her a big hug, everyone praises her dinner. We make several toasts and wish each other happiness in the new millennium.

Then we start to dance like crazy. The phone rings. It's Carlos, wishing us a good start to the millennium. He's watching our party from his box seat.

– Did you talk to Regina? – I ask.

– No, I still have to call her.

We have an unexpected conversation when he tells me that his last dream of the millennium was about me.

– What did you dream? – I want to know.

– I'll tell you later.

– Later when? – I'm very curious.

– When we meet. I've been thinking about you. A lot.

I become quiet and there is an uneasy silence on the telephone.

When Carlos hangs up, I look out the window. Only the light in his bedroom is on. Could he be alone? That's one of the worst experiences someone can have, to be alone on New Year's Eve, particularly for the new millennium. So, I call him:

– Wouldn't you like to bring your guitar?

He arrives shortly, with the guitar under his arm and more bottles of champagne.

Marcelo falls asleep on one of the living room sofas, as expected. Periodically his head falls forward, he opens his eyes slightly, giving the impression that he's awake, then his head falls back again.

I notice Cadu's silence, his deep gaze, and his slow movements. I guess that he isn't participating in the conversation because our words are echoing in his head, a mixture of intimate meanings, brought up from his unconscious by the smoke. Does he feel the same corrosive passion for me that I feel for him?

Suddenly, he starts to take some pictures of all of us, including Lia and Josafá. They enjoy it. They jump from the table to the floor, from the floor to the sofa, and from one lap to the next.

I notice Cadu's insistent and indiscreet stare at Maria Antônia, standing, leaning over the table. I remember Chicão saying that Cadu had a thing for her derrière. I'm jealous. In revenge, Diana relaxes her body and starts to dance furiously with Carlos, who seems happier than ever.

– Beautiful dress – he tells me, his gaze sliding from top to bottom over my body, until he focuses on my fishnet stockings.

Later, while Carlos sings bossa nova and songs by Nelson Gonçalves, Cadu asks me to lie on the sofa, assuming the same position in which he wanted to take my picture a few days ago. Even the position of my face, my legs, everything exactly the same. I think it's funny and obey. I feel undressed by his bold camera.

– A rat! – Cássia yells, hysterical. She climbs up on a chair while our pet rat runs around the corner of the room, headed toward the kitchen, under Josafá's indifferent gaze. We laugh at length and the party becomes livelier.

Carlos is the last to leave. We continue philosophizing, he telling me of the importance of having a companion, a serene love.

– When love is serene, that's because it isn't love – I speculate.

– I'm not talking about lust. But of an abiding friendship between people of the opposite sex – he explains.

When I hear this, I think that, over time, probably the best that remains of a marriage is friendship. It wouldn't be bad to have a friend to sleep with in the same bed, trading caresses and sweet nothings. Even with Chicão I couldn't.

I wanted someone to put me to sleep like daddy did when I was little and bring my teddy bear, leaving it by my head, for me to smell and hug… Would Carlos do this? No, men are always interested in something else.

Cigarette? – he offers.

He lights it for me and we both blow our smoke into the air.

– Look, Ana, Regina fumbled the ball and screwed up the midfield. End of story: our relationship is over. I think it's good, you know? I realize that I wanted to marry her only because I wanted to get married.

The smoke from my cigarette combines with his to form a cloud of tranquility, stationary in the air, tracing distractions. I don't worry about Regina.

– I thought about my resolutions for the new millennium. I want to live at a slow pace, against the tide of contemporary insanity, to take things one at a time – he says. – Because the important thing is to do right, to do enough, and with a clear conscience. One has to take things slowly. To leave room for feelings to grow and mature, it doesn't matter that a maelstrom of things is happening out there. But tell me about you. And your writings?

– It's pretense, you know, to want to summarize everything in my book... It's not made of stone, not at all! It's made of recycled paper. Words can't be kept still when, as you say, the windmill of life spins in this turbulence.

– I believe, precisely, in the constancy of things. You shouldn't quit.

– Look, I stopped reading the newspaper, watching television. That didn't contribute in the slightest to finishing my story. And the meeting of the Useless didn't accomplish the accounting that I wanted to make.

I discover the pleasure of small things, with Carlos at my side, a breeze of emotion blowing in my face, blowing me across the surface of the lake like a paper boat, against the night landscape, made of shades of gray...

– I decided not to move back to Minas. I don't want to see Taimbé again so that I won't be disappointed. I want to keep it intact in my childhood memories.

Carlos makes me feel interesting, when I tell him the most banal scenes from my childhood, awakening early to go to mass and the market with daddy, taking a nap with him and praying the rosary on my knees, with my whole family, before going to bed.

I hear soft notes of an old melody and I don't expect anything, I am susceptible to this night breeze, at the end of the millennium.

– In the present, we never see the flow of time – I say.

– Yes, it's a good thing – Carlos answers, smiling broadly at me.

I see him as an angel beside the cloud of smoke rising from his mouth, a strong mature angel, muscular, nothing like those little Baroque angels that can be seen in the churches of Minas.

Tonight, I feel that the surviving Useless are all still friends. In each of us there is complicity from the old days. We have changed physically and spiritually. But we still trust each other, not because of either common interests or similar ideas. Because we lived through some crises together and together we lost some of the same things. We dreamed the same unfulfilled dreams. I recognize something artificial in this enduring friendship: we have all changed and, despite that, in relation to each other it's as if we were frozen in time, seeing each other not with today's eyes but rather with eyes of thirty years ago. We don't remake our relationships based on who we are; we play out our old relationships, or more precisely, our idealized relationships.

We missed Berta. Maybe she just wanted to sever contact with us. Her absence is my fault. I offended her because of my prejudices, Chicão got it right, I have to admit. The main thing missing was the elevation, the epiphany that could overcome daily banality, returning us to the magical gathering of thirty years ago and reminding us that the new millennium was arriving. Chicão is right, everything will remain the same. Only the days pass, one after another, with the permanence of things good and bad, and with changes for better and for worse.

Thinking about Cadu, I realize that frustration is the last name of desire. And what's more, that a man's love doesn't matter. I will feel love for plants, animals, my niece and nephew… I don't want anything more to do with loving a man. Saying goodnight to Carlos at the door, I smell jasmine and, in spite of everything, I feel a certain sense of inner peace.

It's a shame that it would never work out with Carlos. I'm too somber for him. In spite of his agreeable disposition, he would never be interested in me, except perhaps as a friend.

I should cultivate my friendship with him. It's funny that he would think of love as friendship between people of the opposite sex... Maybe he sees me as a sister... He has a sister in Brasília whom he almost never sees.

The men not loved, the books not written, the places not visited, the experiences not had, the things not possessed, the life not lived exist inside me with the same energy as all that I loved, saw, had and lived, but only in the imaginary territory that consumes me and is as real as its opposite. For the first time I accept the losses and absences in my life, like the fact that I will always be alone. It's a relief – and it makes me happy – to think of myself as a self-sufficient, confirmed single woman. I don't know whether I should call it old age or maturity not to expect anything more, to tame ambition and desire, to convince myself that my life is the past, love is the past, and in the past it wasn't love; sex is in the past and the past doesn't count, it's good for nothing, a past of no importance, of no note to anyone. I don't live in the past, but in the present, and by embracing the present that I live in I am only who I am, I don't want, neither can I be anything else; I don't need anything, I won't have anything, all told I don't owe anything to anyone, I am due nothing more except perhaps the life that I'm living. Whatever else comes is pure profit, friendship with Carlos, perhaps.

My resolution for the millennium is to finish the destruction of the papers in a dramatic fashion: fast and final. I have to rid myself of this weight, to begin the new century, as Carlos says, with a cleansed spirit. Tomorrow will be a full day: going to the cemetery in the morning, lunch at Japona's restaurant and a dinner given by Chicão.

A small green insect crawls across the fronds of the fern. It appears here to complete my thought. It's an insect commonly known as hope. It must be nonsense for me to believe in these coincidences, in this simple symbology. This hope must have a meaning for me, on this first day of the millennium. As small as might be, as much as I may try to deny it and recognize it as pure illusion, hope dares to survive. Without it, what present could I possibly endure?

5

THE LAST SEASON OF LOVE

Everything that one is, everything that one builds year after year, can be lost in an instant when the Devil intervenes. It is well known that haste is the enemy of perfection, and no better outcome could be expected from a creation that took only seven days to consummate. God was dissatisfied and in a foul mood when He made man.

The Devil had his eye on me. *Diabolos*, the one who makes lateral incursions. I only learn of his work the morning after Chicão's dinner. January 2nd, Sunday, I learn of the heinous crime. The victim's body, punctured by dozens of knife wounds, was found by a street cleaner in a gutter in the area of Planaltina. Near the almost naked body, a purse with no money, containing the ID card. When I read that it's Mona Habib, the daughter of some as yet unlocated Lebanese couple, I ask Chicão to please contact the police, because I panic at the police, Chicão knows that. Together we later make the identification of Berta's transfigured body at the police morgue. A horrible shock!

I have said it before and I repeat: it's possible to lose in an instant not only what one has constructed year after year, but also everything that one is, because what will remain of Berta other than the crime, the evil, the infamy? And why associate a name with this? I wished the Philosopher were here to explain why "only death is complete and perfect…"

Two detectives come to see me. They ask me to identify any suspects. I don't know of any suspects. I think about what Berta told me that night she cried on my shoulder; the one she had loved the most was the one she had feared the most. Could it have been a crime of passion?

– She must have gone with strangers, not thinking what they could be capable of – I tell the detectives.

They ask me to describe the necklaces and bracelets that Berta might have been wearing. I tell them about my pistol, as well.

I am a sleepwalker in the funeral procession where life hides, here and there, always small and fragile. I grope along the cars in the procession imagined by the Philosopher. I look under them in the hope of seeing Berta again. I still want to tell her that I like her. That I'm sorry she left. That I wish her the best. To warn her that the world out there is very dangerous.

I have no way of locating a living soul in Berta's family, except her son Luís. For the first time I talk with his mother, Carolina, who is distraught. I reach the Useless with the news.

Although the police report leaves no doubts about the *causa mortis,* Berta's body is only released after an autopsy. We argue – Chicão, Japona, and I – about the possibility of embalming the body to extend the time for the wake. We finally decide on cremation. So the body goes to the crematory oven on Tuesday morning when, in spite of being kept in the refrigerator, it's already in the early stages of decomposition. In the afternoon, we hold a simple ceremony at the cemetery.

There is a sad beauty in the air. It's the second time in two days that we had come to the cemetery. The morning of the day before we had taken flowers to Eva's grave and there remembered the deceased Useless.

Some particularly colorful butterflies accompany us, and Carlos is the one who points them out to me. It's just the Useless, two journalists interested in the crime, Marcelo, Carlos, Berenice, Carolina, Luís, Formiga, and Vera. Judging by the gentleness of her face, Carolina – fat and lacking in charm – must have been pretty once.

It's the rainy season. The sky is black. I imagine that a sheet of rain may fall, as it did on the day that we ate mushrooms and held hands, receiving a mysterious energy. The rain doesn't fall, nor do we hold hands, or even speak to each other. I cry uncontrollable tears as if a dam had broken. They are torrents washing my face of the most complete despair.

– If I ever come across the son of a bitch who did this to Berta, he won't escape – I threaten, sobbing.

Then Carlos comes over and hugs my shoulders. I feel as if he were my father; a paternal touch is just what I need. An ideal father, who doesn't censure what I say, what I feel, or what I do.

The other women cry too. The men don't. I notice Chicão's profoundly sad look. I propose that we join hands. Then Maria Antônia makes a speech. She talks about the friendship that unites us, a friendship that is here in the air we breathe and that will always unite us wherever we are, no matter what might happen. She says that Berta's spirit of adventure was an expression of her unrestrained love of life, that the tragedy of her death should mark the beginning of a campaign for human rights, that she has gone to join the perspicacity of the Philosopher and the romanticism of Eva and Helena. For all of us, Eva is a true symbol of the 70s. And Helena had died for causes that are still alive. We remain a few minutes longer holding hands, listening to the song of the birds that flock overhead.

I maintain my composure until everyone says goodbye. Back home before the urn containing Berta's ashes, small and pretty as a jewelry box, I feel a great despondency.

– It's over, there's no point attempting anything else – I sob to Berenice. Berta was an important part of me. Without her I'm just half.

I really am a petit bourgeois bitch. It's my fault. Chicão was right to talk of my moralism. Instead of giving Berta tenderness, reciprocating her attention, I forced her to run away. All she ever wanted was to have someone, to be someone… I threw her to the lions.

When I retire to my room, I encounter the last boxes of writings that I haven't had time to empty. I have no energy left to continue this Sisyphean task that increases the weight on my mind rather than relieving it. I stop at a page from my forties, soon after my separation from Eduardo. Although everything had happened exactly as I hoped, with the exception of my separation, I felt I had failed in every aspect of my life – in love, sex, and work – and I attributed this to the lack of pleasure in what I was doing. Rereading the page, I think that I would be more relaxed if I had been raised in an ascetic environment, instead of succumbing to a hedonistic vision that considered all pleasure insufficient. And the idea of abandoning my material wealth, my friends, the pursuit of pleasure, and retiring to some convent occurs to me. I could be a good nun. Like in the medieval monasteries, I could dedicate the rest of my life to a meticulous, perfect task, in this case the destruction of the rest of the papers and the conclusion of the definitive book. Declaring myself already cloistered, I tell Berenice that I don't want to see anyone and I won't take calls.

From the living room picture window, a starless sky, a flat landscape, the garden green and unkempt… I'm exhausted, as I was when I caught that virus almost a year ago. This time I mean it, I'll never leave the house again. Not even my room, or my bed. *If I wanted, I could go crazy.*

I surprise Rodolfo with a book in his mouth. He seems to revert to the old days when he pulled books off the shelf to chew. I imagine that chance, which is God and the Devil combined, is plotting to tell me something through Rodolfo. I take the book from his mouth and open it at random. My eyes light on one of the strophes from 1483, in the *Cancioneiro português*, that glosses sad passions, and I focus on one verse: *Es el remedio morir.* A random sentence, in the midst of insignificant writing, that reminds me of another sentence: *Un bel morire tutta una vita onora.* Words that come from such a distance, if they still say anything to me, tell me more about the present than about the world from which they come. It's the state I'm in that lends them special significance.

I wanted a revolution? The arrival of my hour of truth? My pleas were heard, only by Satan, the adversary. I'm mired in a mudhole of anguish. In my condition, if they study the chemicals my brain is producing, they'll invent a vaccine for melancholy and unhappiness. Of the millions of words piled against my bedroom walls, I pick up only those echoing in my head: *Es el remedio morir*, a message that arrives from the fifteenth century with the weight of history to dictate my death at the end of the millennium.

– Mister Carlos is here, Miss Ana. He wants to see you, Ma'am – Berenice tells me.

I think about the hug he gave me, but I don't have the strength to get up:

– I don't want to see anyone, absolutely no one, Berenice.

Locked in my room I feel like a rag. I've already done everything I had to do. I wasn't recognized for anything. And my few friends are going to remember me as… useless! No promise of enlightenment surrounding me, the shadow of death darkens the landscape where my imagination reposes.

On Friday a detective comes to see me.

– Ma'am, do you recognize this weapon? – He pulls out my revolver.

Following an anonymous tip, the police located one of Berta's alleged murderers, one Jefferson José Ramos, Fefé, who had this revolver registered to me in his possession. A statement that I lent the weapon to Berta is required. At the police station I sign documents for the revolver to be used as evidence against Fefé and, at the end, I get it back, taking advantage of the fact that the prohibition against carrying weapons hasn't gone into effect. I go back to keeping it in the customary place, atop the wardrobe.

On Saturday I go to the seventh day mass for Berta's soul in the little church in block 307. It's the first time in years that I set foot in church. Maria Antônia and Cadu have already left town, Japona couldn't come, so it's just me, Carlos, Chicão, Carolina, Vera, and Luís here. In the geometry of the blue and white tiles, my thoughts wander over the moments spent with Berta. She had guided this past year of mine, created the expectation of the millennium reunion, and indirectly led me to revolutionize my life with the help of the destruction of my papers and the composition of my as yet unfinished story. After mass, I refuse Carlos' invitation to lunch.

Back home, kneeling, I say out loud the St. Judas Thaddeus prayer for hopeless cases, the prayer that Berenice read on the day of the attempted robbery, and a copy of which Berta gave me later:

– "St. Jude, glorious apostle, faithful servant and friend of Jesus, the name of the traitor has caused you to be forgotten by many. But the Church honors and invokes you universally as the patron of hopeless cases, and of things despaired of. Pray for me who am so distressed. Make use, I implore you, of that particular privilege accorded you to bring visible and speedy help where help was almost despaired of. Come to my assistance in this great need that I may receive the consolation and succor of Heaven in all my necessities, tribulations and sufferings, particularly..." – At this point it says: "here make your particular request." Then I ask: – "to find a meaning for my life..." And I go on with the prayer to the end: – "and that I may bless God with you and all the elect throughout eternity. St. Jude, apostle, martyr, and relative of our Lord Jesus Christ, of Mary, and of Joseph, intercede for us! Amen."

Then I see how ridiculous this is, it's my despair that brings me to this position. Wasn't that the prayer Berta was carrying in her purse when the unfathomable tragedy occurred? There's no point in being superstitious, or believing in fairies, saints, miracles. There's no way out, from here on it's all downhill.

The following day, I tell Berenice to enjoy her Sunday; she always spends her weekends in the Bandeirante Settlement. She hesitates, wanting to keep me company. I insist that I don't need anything and prefer to be alone. Formiga and Vera have gone out.

This sad and ugly Sunday afternoon, when it's been a week since I learned of Berta's death in the newspapers, I first decide to throw out the laptop on which I was writing the definitive story that no longer makes any sense and in no way substitutes for the stored papers. Only additional words piled up. I look through the letters sent by Berta, or rather, Norberto, from São Paulo, Paris, and the last of them, from San Francisco, this one talking about his return and mentioning the reunion of the Useless. I leave them on the desk. Then I assure myself that Formiga and Vera haven't returned yet. I put Rodolfo out. He's in the garden crying to come back in, but I don't take pity on him.

My soul is dead, the only thing that remains is to kill my body. *Es el remedio morir.* I get the revolver from atop the wardrobe. For an instant I still recall the adventure that brought me to the Central Plateau, as if to fulfill a mission. It occurs to me that from the beginning the monumental structure of Brasília defined the limits of that adventure of mine. I see myself outside the walls of a medieval castle. *Un bel morire tutta una vita onora.* Why shouldn't a death by choice be a worthy solution, in this open prison, contemplating these walls?

I look for the extra bullets in the dresser drawer. I load the gun. I take a sheet of paper from the various piles that have accumulated in my room. Curiously, it's a commentary on selfishness, based on a selection from St. Augustine that goes something like this: the earthly city was made from love of self to the detriment of God. Should I still pay attention to words that I come across by chance? I certainly want to kill myself out of selfishness. Not for love of self but rather for uncontained hatred of self. Because I can't be what I want. For cowardice, and also because I didn't keep myself young. I'm either everything or nothing.

Survive for the sake of others? No one is going to miss me, not even Chicão. Life is neither more beautiful nor more sublime than death. "To each a death, according to his or her life. Only death is complete and perfect…"

This is my revolt, my revolution. Enough mediocre acceptance of this existence. If there were a bomb here, I would blow up the house, Brasília, the world, this work by an ill-tempered God.

I set fire to this sheet of paper. And the fire spreads to the remaining papers, to the incomplete story, to the love pile. I have the feeling that the bonfire will replace kilos of paper with a spiritual essence that I see here in the smoke. I want to set fire to everything, the house, myself.

I see the rat, my companion during this past year, escaping out the door. It was hiding behind the papers and flees the heat of the fire. Then I feel the fire invading the whole atmosphere. I want to die before it burns me.

On the brink of disaster a lake a flower that blossoms dead red clouds that interrogate me a mere shadow of desire's misadventures a painting and embrace of abandonment time's impurities the image of the past in motion and the terror-stricken gaze of the angel looking back at the ruins A hollow center awakens sleeping gods a new law of causality manifests itself freely in the snare of insanity Abyss in a fold of thought when framing the landscape on the edge Paranoá Lake blade now mirroring despair This flower essence of my anguish My shadow in this landscape in the painting on the wall painting of an absence. I grab the revolver, point it at my ear and fire.

When I regain consciousness, I see a crucifix high on the white wall before me. Machines blink around me, hanging liquids bring medication to my veins and I smell the strong hospital odor. At my side are Alaíde, Eduardo's wife, Mom, Regina, my niece and nephew, and Rui. There are also flowers and cards on a table.

Before me, a brief film with each character presented in short flashes: "My little girl," Mother says, syrupy, stroking my hair. "You had surgery, but you'll recover quickly," I hear Regina, who later tells me that she, Mother and my niece and nephew are staying with Chicão. "Hi, Auntie," Vera smiles. "You have many friends who love you," Alaíde tells me slowly, clearly enunciating the words with her stuttering voice. She's perfectly right to treat me like a crazy woman. Only Formiga is circumspect, he looks at me as if he doesn't believe I'm alive.

As soon as he heard the news, Rui caught a plane to Brasília. As shy as he is, he tries to babble something. It's just as well that he can't. The letters that he wrote to me are already ashes, but here he is before me, in flesh and blood. He's so sweet... He's as ugly as ever, and unfortunately I find him boring and so sad that it makes me sadder still and sharpens the pain that I feel not just where I had surgery, but also on the burns on my arms, back, and legs. This unfair reaction to so much goodness is so physical, or more precisely so chemical, that I can't control it. I'm nice to him, a distant proper politeness, but his prolonged presence makes me impatient. He understands, because he says that he's only going to stay one day.

The doctor explains that the bullet had lodged behind my brain, that I was nearly paralyzed and mentally damaged. I assume that I was saved because my hand was unsteady and also because Carlos, upon hearing the shot, didn't hesitate to break into my house and remove me from the bedroom in flames. I know for sure now why I have seen him as an angel; he truly is my guardian angel. "You need to thank that gentleman," Mother says. He had spent several hours at the hospital while I was unconscious.

Jeremias and several other former university colleagues had called. The flowers on the table were sent by someone named Cleuza. I understand, when I read the card, that she's the woman with the cat in the freezer. I saved her life, she writes, she didn't commit suicide only on my account, I gave her back the will to live, she had found out about me from the vet. I become alarmed at the mention of his name, but Formiga assures me that Rodolfo is fine, after treatment for the burns he suffered when he tried to follow Carlos in search of me. The whole house was destroyed, he says, and the fire even reached the garage, where my car exploded.

In these first few hours after regaining consciousness, I have a visit from Cadu and Joana. My heart still races when I see him. It would be better to be dead than to have this awareness of an unrequited passion. He's a shit, a son of a bitch, for him it's as if nothing had happened between us. It's my problem, I grant him forgiveness. And here he is, pleasant, smiling, the son of a bitch. His affair with Joana is one of the most successful I know, perhaps because they never lived together. It even survived Joana's marriage. She told me once that marriage ruins the pleasure of relationships.

Cadu brings me the photographs – all in black and white – from our party of the Useless. One of them, enlarged to 24 x 30 cm, is of me. Although here I am very well dressed, I'm in the same position that he had wanted to photograph me only days earlier. That's why I see myself as if I were reclining on a divan in a North Wing apartment partially wrapped in a sheet. The photo highlights my body, whose curves seem to be more willowy than they are, and also my face, wearing a sensual melancholy smile. With the photo, Cadu leaves me two cigarettes as a gift. "I rolled them with love. They're top quality and are good for relieving pain," he tells me.

Maria Antônia calls from São Paulo. She understands how I feel, she is and will always be there for me, I should always count on her; when I'm up to it, why don't I spend some time in São Paulo? There's room in her apartment.

But the call that makes me happiest is the one from my niece Juliana. She has recovered and can even run.

– Why don't you spend your vacation with us, Auntie?

– Because now I have an endless vacation, Juliana. I'm on vacation until I die. And then I'll have an eternal vacation.

– Well, I only have two months.

In the late afternoon they announce Cleuza, the cat woman. I thank her for the flowers. She has the same tragic Greek face from when I met her, and she's still wearing black. She speaks from her deep black eyes:

– I know we're not close enough for me to pay this call, so I want to apologize. But I want to be sure that you're all right, that you want to live…

I almost confess that I wish I had died. I keep silent. I'm in pain, I don't want to think about life, death, the future, or anything at all.

– I've been through trying situations and know how important it is to have someone close by to trust – Cleuza goes on.

That day when we met by chance, the vet had disclosed who I was. That meeting had been very important, she was on the brink of suicide not only because of the cat, but also and mainly because of the vet, who was her boyfriend then, and is still a friend.

– He gave me another beautiful sweet cat, you know?

It's already dark when Marcelo and Chicão arrive. Chicão gives me a miniature of the Our Lady of Hope that Cabral brought on his voyage and whose original is in Belmonte, Portugal. Like me, he's not religious. That's why his gesture moves me even more.

– This is a treasure, Chicão. Thank you very much – I say, although I think I need to banish hope from my life.

Marcelo also tries to raise my spirits:

– You're wrong to say that hope is the last to die. It never dies.

I thank them for taking in my mother, Regina, and my niece and nephew.

– Only a true friend would do it – I say.

– You know you're my sister – Chicão says as he leaves. – Whatever you need, practical arrangements, to play canasta, whatever, just tell me.

I fall asleep watching the television news: wars, crises, murders, hunger, the same old misery. At night, I wake with Carlos' warm eyes watching me. With flowers in hand, he says that we are kindred spirits. He sits next to me. Eventually, he confesses that, if I need to, I can stay with him as long as I want. That his house also has room for Vera and Formiga. Berenice, the cats and Rodolfo, in fact, are already there.

My heart can't find the words it seeks. It stutters and goes quiet. Should I ask Diana to wake me, to dare say the ineffable, which I can only guess? In a frail condition, feeling lacerated inside, I calmly spill tears from my eyes. I know that "thank you" is not appropriate for this occasion. I am limited to it because nothing better occurs to me.

– Look, Ana, advance the ball! – he recites his refrain.

– My dear, he cares a great deal for you – Mother says after Carlos leaves.

– Do you think he's a good catch? – I jokingly ask her.

– He's a gentleman. And, from what I've seen, from what he did for you, I have no doubt that he really likes you. You'll learn over time that the most important thing is to find someone who can take care of us with tenderness and that we can trust. And if we don't find that person at the right time, then it's too late.

I think about marriages in times past, arranged by the parents and wrapped in religion. If my marriage to Eduardo had been arranged, perhaps love would have been born and grown with our intimacy. Left to ourselves, the process reversed. Eduardo and I were free of the weight and also the help of family and religion. We married for love. Our mistake was believing that the love that freely chose marriage could, by itself, give meaning to life. I spent years thinking that Eduardo was annoyed by my affection… Intimacy threw cold water on the flame that had once united us.

Lying in my hospital bed, I understand the meaning of the word catastrophe, *katastrophê*, as the Greeks used to say, reversal, commotion, ruin. If a life changes due to external factors, mine is suddenly radically different. I'm in the hospital, Berta dead, all my papers incinerated. Ashes, carbonized emotions, return to dust.

On the one hand, the lack of papers brings relief and gives me a feeling of freedom. I am now only a body abandoned to the world, with an idle spirit, a spirit that doesn't need to carry forward any written word. Written words no longer constrain my beliefs or my knowledge. On the other hand, my confused history, which I will never understand, is not erased. Even out of the ashes, its forms will continue to appear. What I destroy persists in the negation of what once existed. No, nothing disappears without leaving a trace. Even palimpsests remain on the computer that I threw in the trash and whose whereabouts I do not know.

Being homeless is not freedom, having nowhere to go isn't either. It's a good thing I still have my history and my family. I wanted zero, but zero is only leftover past. This time Regina and Mother are right to want to take me to Taimbé. And if I leave, Berenice might go back to Ceará or stay permanently working for Carlos.

Vera tells me that she's finally going to live with Luís. I find no arguments to oppose her and even Regina finally agrees, not without first giving her advice about the necessity of going to college and of postponing any plans to have children.

In less than two weeks I am released and settle into Chicão's apartment, while mother and Regina go on to Taimbé. Even though she likes Carlos, Mother is against the idea that I live with him for no reason, without even plans to date – and she's right. I would love Carlos for everything he did for me and for all his qualities. I enjoy seeing him, talking to him, having him by my side, always in a good mood. But I'm unable to love him. Unless love, contrary to what I believe, can grow by rational will. Maybe it's possible. Everything grows slowly, from seed – the only instantaneous change is the one that separates life from death. And the seed exists: it's the affection that I feel for his kindness; the gratitude for his generosity; the admiration for his patience; even the attraction for his gentle gestures emerging from a large muscular physique. Above all, I'm pleased that he likes flowers.

It's a passing fancy. If I married Carlos, I would soon discover that he's not this tender appearance. He would share his problems with me, perhaps his kidney pains. The spiritual beauty that he communicates would be obscured by his bad breath when he awakes, by the exposed face of an ill-tempered male chauvinist. At my age, I'm not about to share a roof with a man, to wear myself out with him in daily routine. At our age, we're already set in our ways, and men are very different from women. If only I were in love... Yes, Berta was my lost opportunity to have a stable companion, settled into an unfettered friendship. It was her arrival that opened me up to a new life; it was her death that carried me to the abyss. She crossed my life like a river, dividing it in two.

– Ana, you're marvelous – Carlos says about nothing at all, a few days before my departure, when I arrive at his house to thank him for everything he did and to visit my animals. I fear that Rodolfo won't last much longer. He's too old to handle the suffering caused by all these changes... The worst thing for him is the absence of Vera, to whom he was so attached.

I see the few things that Carlos courageously saved from the fire. The picture that Berta did of me is one of them. Carlos grabbed if off the living room wall when he went into the house the second time to remove what he thought was most valuable. He also saved my gold lighter, a gift from Eduardo. What I don't even want to see right now is my revolver, which Carlos has already hidden. From the living room, the pots survived the fire along with the china in the cabinet, which he also did me the favor of keeping.

I ask him to visit the burned house with me. It's not masochism, I want to face the situation with open eyes. I'm sure that afterwards I'll feel better. We weren't able to keep Rodolfo from following us. "Be careful! There are places where the ceiling may still collapse," Carlos warns as we enter the ruins, which doesn't dissuade me from walking through almost the whole house. In my bedroom, I stumble on a group of philosophers fallen from charred boxes, disintegrating into ashes like their stories. It's as if I could see: the vanguard of the proletariat, the philosophy of history… The forecasts of decadence or progress are wasted. The unpredictable is possible and it jumps, twisted and tortured, from path to path, leaving its marks on the evolution of human history. I should enrich my theory of instantaneism.

In the living room, the furniture though ruined is recognizable. There is a spot of red beneath the coffee table. It's the Chinese figurine Berta gave me. I also find intact the little bottle of soil collected during the trip to the Garden of Salvation. Berta's ashes, however, are mixed with the others, leaving no trace. They are nothing now, like the nothing created in me. I think about my childhood and the small ash cross that the priest used to make on my forehead. Ashes, carbonized emotions, a return to dust. What life can still be born from this dust of mourning? I touch my fingers to the ashes that cover the floor, ashes of my house, ashes that should be of my body, ashes of my dead soul, and Berta's ashes, and I gently spread them over the creases in my face, as if they were rouge. To lighten the gravity of my gesture, I tell Carlos in an ordinary tone:

– My plan is to sell this lot and buy my own house in Taimbé with the money.

Carlos laughs at my black mask. When we return to the house, it's not enough for him to clean my face tenderly with a wet towel.

Like Rodolfo, I am covered with ashes from top to bottom. We have fun bathing Rodolfo with the garden hose. As for me, I can't go out like this, I ask Carlos for permission to take a shower, and I also wash the figurine. When I say goodbye, he asks again if I'm sure I want to go back to a small town in Minas, it would give him great pleasure to take me in "until *the ash* settles."

— I didn't accept his invitation because it wouldn't look right — I tell Chicão later.

— You still have last millennium prudishness — he comments. — But you can also stay with Marcelo and me as long as you like.

At last I get ready for the trip to Taimbé, which I haven't visited since my twenties. The change will do me good. Brasília is the heavy streaks of rain on the window, the noisy cars passing, the loneliness of a big city, death, unrequited love, anguish… I remember stories of a return to the point of departure — which means the recuperation of lost values, honor, dignity, the reencounter with truth and purity, the rediscovery of authenticity and of true friendship — that are woven on sidewalks and at dinner tables of small towns in the countryside. With old age, the moment comes when we need to support ourselves by our roots. Zero, a new beginning. That a new branch of me may grow from the ashes — tremulous, fragile, but resolved to live. There I am, enveloped in telluric feelings, thinking that my very blood sprouted from Taimbé, and that my spirit was breathed forth by the mountains encircling it. I, who only drink *cachaça* in caipirinhas, discover the advantages of having easier access to Taimbé's cachaça. I fantasize conversations on the verandah with childhood friends and walks through the brush, breathing the pure air, hearing birds sing, accumulating wisdom and peacefully living an eternity. My family is the uterus that awaits me. I want to be near my father's grave, hear the night voices of a small town, awake early to go to the market, even, who knows, go back to attending mass on Sunday.

I even dream about the house of my childhood. It's a baptism party for one of my dolls. I don't recognize some of the guests. Carlos is there, Paulinho, and also Regina. The baptism is for my doll Felipe, a china doll that has just broken his neck and looks like he's been decapitated. I hold his head in my hand, to which the baptismal gown is still attached. I go into the garden and try to bury it. Felipe's eyes stubbornly live on and look at me wide open. Then I dig deeper into the manure whose stench bothers me and, when I'm finally making Felipe disappear into the hole, the neighbors look at me from the building next door – a building that is now part of a Brasília superblock – they think me guilty of Felipe's death, I'm going to be arrested. I wake with an intense anxiety, convinced that a vivid dream like this doesn't hide how much Taimbé is inside of me, and how much I need to return there.

To my surprise, Formiga is eager to go with me. Initially my idea is that he'll just help me take Rodolfo and the cats, then I'll see if it's possible to keep him in Brasília. I don't want the move to interfere with his studies.

Before we leave, I accept his suggestion to retrieve the revolver from Carlos' house to sell. Formiga gets only one hundred reais for the weapon and even asks me to keep the money.

It's difficult to leave Chicão and Berenice. They're the two people I will miss most. I ask Carlos to keep for now the things that one day he'll send to Taimbé. Rodolfo, Lia, and Josafá are going with us. The trip is expensive, with the costs covered by the last of my savings, besides being long and tiring, first by plane to Belo Horizonte, then by bus to Montes Claros, where Regina comes in her car to get us. From there we climb the Espinhaço Range until we descend in the direction of the headwaters of the Vacaria River, where I can recognize the landscape of my childhood. Taimbé is near here.

I arrive with my few things, innumerable practical arrangements to be made and the intention of ending my days in this place. I recognize the market and the Church of Our Lady of the Rosary. The streets are more full of people and cars, the sun shines brightly and it is very hot. Mother still lives in the same house where I was born, that now looks dwarfed.

Within days, I become the local attraction, complete with the right to an exaggerated space in the social columns of the *Taimbé Daily*. The curious go by our sidewalk just to see me. Even strangers come to visit. We talk about Brasília, this year's harvests and who has been born, died, moved or married. Poorer relations, not knowing of my problems, come to ask for help. Mother and Regina didn't tell anyone about my house fire or the real reason for my surgery. They disseminated the version – with my collusion, of course – that I was in a car accident.

I spend the day imagining how life with no other occupation than being polite to strangers and keeping house with Mother and Regina is possible, while listening to suggestions on how to be or not to be. I miss having a bidet in the minuscule bathroom that I have to share, no less, with Regina. I store my creams in the bedroom closet. Some of these problems certainly will be solved when I have my own house. I'm invited to attend a rodeo, spend a weekend at the ranch of some distant cousins, breathe the fresh air of the mountains and appreciate the view from the eastern slopes of the Espinhaço Range. I like the climate at this time of year, the quality of the water and the cachaça, the fruit preserves, market smells and even the stench of horse manure in the streets. Everything as I expected.

This love affair with the place doesn't last long. After two weeks, I'm not entirely apathetic only because I start to miss my papers, which makes me uneasy. It's as if I couldn't live without them and as if the life that I wanted to throw away continued here, stubborn, starved for words. I even take up the idea of the narrative again. It would be different now, totally different, centered on the story of an old child, me, who revolts because the world around her has changed. I buy paper that I take from one place to another and that remains blank, just like when I had the writer's block that led me to tear up my accumulated writings to compose the stone book.

The void increases, the absence... Absence of I know-not-what, I know-not-whom. The absence of Berta, who returned to Brasília to prove that I'm incomplete, that I can't survive alone, and also how ephemeral that stone book would have been. My new writing should deal with everything that's happened to me ever since Berta announced her arrival.

For the first time I feel Carlos' absence also. I think I've lost an opportunity for a friendship that would have something new to teach me; that could transport me across some frontier. I would be happy if I saw his face again, heard his measured voice, or his laugh.

– What's with you? – Regina asks, when she notices that I have been distracted.

– Nothing – I answer, disguising my sadness with difficulty. – I can't stay here with you two forever, can I? I need to put my life in order.

One day Rodolfo wakes up vomiting. There's only one veterinarian in town. He's out in the field, caring for horses. When he arrives, there's no hope left. It looks like Rodolfo was poisoned. We bury him in the backyard. It would've already been my fourth burial in the space of a year, if we had also held one for my cat Leo. I write to Carlos telling him my routine and giving the sad news.

Two weeks later, on my birthday, he calls to congratulate me. He misses me. He's going to get up the courage to say what he would've liked to have said long ago. He wants me to be his girlfriend, he says right out, as long as the courtship is brief. What he really wants is to ask me to marry him. He continues in a crescendo, until declaring that he could come get me immediately. My departure had left him with an enormous void.

I remember the red rose he gave me a year ago, the fragile petals against his muscular torso, picked especially for me, on that afternoon in which the red clouds rose through the sky questioning me. Ever since then, everything has been a detour; I would have taken a shortcut to happiness, I think, if I had released my Diana side that afternoon.

This time I don't cringe from the unexpected. On the contrary, I can seize the moment to act fully on what has arrived out of the blue. I spent years living a kind of starved love, the child of penury, described by Diotima in the *Banquet* and commented in a selection that is part of my library ashes, a love fated to the incessant search for what it lacks and, therefore, for possession and suffering; a love in search of the good and beautiful, which it never attains, because what it achieves always eludes it. The moment to love the attainable has arrived.

– If I stay here one more month I'll die – I answer Carlos, in all sincerity.

I don't need to think, it's as if I'd known him forever, living with him is not only possible, it's the best thing that can happen to me.

I don't know if Diana agrees with me or if I agree with her, if what matters is my chosen name or the one on paper, I don't know which of us is more daring, which is more deliberate, we share reason and heart as sisters. I have to be myself, whole, complete, reconciling my divisions, arming myself against death, in favor of life.

When Carlos arrives in Taimbé, I tremble inside with the loving kiss and the long embrace that he gives me. I cry from so much emotion. I'm prepared to renounce everything, even myself, just because I want to. I want to love without relying on reciprocity. Is feeling this way a beginning of love? Does love have beginnings? Or could it be that I only want someone who can lie beside me and keep me company? With whom I can talk about the wild meadow plants? Who will show me the butterflies? Who will describe the sky and point out the Southern Cross? Who will take up his guitar and sing bossa nova and Nelson Gonçalves' songs for me? Who will give me news of what's happening in the world, bring me flowers, and declare that we are twin souls…

They say one doesn't love by trying to love, that love comes by its own paths, independent of our decision, that it arrives with no prior notice, but what I really want is to love, to be open to Carlos, to be tender with him. As if I were about to jump from a springboard, the initial impulse is mine, I decide whether to jump or not, no one pushes me, nor do I move in that direction like a sleepwalker not knowing my destination. My legs neither deceive me, nor am I unconscious. I walk to the end of the springboard because I choose to; I jump of my own free will, not for some uncontrollable desire or attraction...

I reach the end of the springboard and jump, done. I want to freefall and I know that gravity will carry me down. No point in trying to reverse my course in midair. Here I go throwing myself, to fall freely for love and in love. And what if I'm alone in this freefall? And what if Carlos panics and runs? Could it be that my distance and coldness are what attract him? And even if he thinks he likes me, what will happen when he sees the wounds from my burns and scars and thinks about how much insanity I have inside me?

I don't know how to tell him that it's the fear inside of me that wants him. That it's my weariness that seeks his shoulder. That it's the loneliness inside of me that feels attracted like a magnet to his loneliness. Each of my parts, my affection and my misfortune, the disappointments and the hope, the child who loved Paulinho, my sins and my virtues, seeks him. Could this attempt to find friendship with someone who attracts me with his goodness and beauty be love?

So, I revise my theory of instantaneism. Things evolve in many directions, but there are moments in which the whole of them presents itself harmoniously from an unexpected perspective. Sometimes, looking in a new direction, we discover that the confusion settles. There are too many things in the world, and it's always possible to find a way to assemble them into a given shape. And one single thing becomes many. Like I once saw at an exhibition, a sculpture had a radically different appearance, depending on the angle from which it was possible to view it. We are certain only of what we see from that angle, in a given instant that is also woven of illusions, memories, and imagined lives. Well then, before I used to be indecisive and thought that only questioning was worthwhile. I wanted to undo everything. Now I refuse to think that everything is nothing. I'm no longer certain that it's better to live by questions and indecision, to predict that everything is unpredictable, to determine that everything is indeterminate. On the contrary, everything can be affirmed in the eternity of an instant, when I recompose the whole in a specific way. Everything, the whole. One must analyze the instant from the angle that contains all angles at the same time, in order to discern its clear crystalline form. I no longer believe in seizing the instant to deny the flow of time. I prefer an emotional agreement, a negotiation suffered through adversity, the courage to continue clearing trails through the fields of existence, instead of abandoning everything in the hope of finding paradise. Because paradise was splintered and its remains lost in the dust of time, only here and there do we come across its crumbs that we can collect, like objets trouvés… I want to embrace each fragment of existence and not an empty whole, to discover the possibility hidden in each inert thing, in each life, in each movement, the chance to build and rebuild with what is here, instead of searching for what doesn't exist and cannot exist.

For all these reasons I decide to say yes – or perhaps *these reasons* are the consequence and not the cause of my yes. The wedding is held right here in Taimbé in the Church of Our Lady of the Rosary, to satisfy Mother. The ceremony is attended by her, Regina, a few relatives and friends of the family, in addition to the crowds of curious.

Even though Carlos invited Formiga to come with us to Brasília, he prefers to stay behind. To my surprise, he has grown to like Taimbé. In Brasília his studies were going downhill and, since he was able to get a place in a school in Taimbé, I think it's not a bad idea for him to keep Mother and Regina company.

Arriving in Brasília, Carlos and I get married in a civil ceremony in the presence of Chicão and Marcelo – godparents on my side – Japona, Cássia, Mônica, Vera, Luís, Berenice, Carlos' sister, who lives in Brasília and I'm only now meeting, a couple of Carlos' former colleagues from the Congressional Library – godparents on his side – besides Cleuza, the crazy woman with the dead cat, who I couldn't prevent from coming, after Carlos' indiscretion about our wedding when he took Lia to the vet.

On my first day with Carlos on the terrace of his house, our house, this landscape may be similar to many others I've seen, but the skies now traveling over the surface of the lake and reflected in it are tinged with joy. It's a sign of my new times. I'm here in a calm that I've never felt, with my two cats and Berenice, observing the gorgeous autumn afternoon.

I look back and what I see is an obvious truth: nothing in life is easy, not even love, which must be constructed; there's joy along with sorrow, pleasure together with pain; distance is needed to perceive the shape that life takes while it's being woven into stitches, into lace, across a surface that is never smooth, that moves with the wind and with what lies beneath, that mirrors what flies overhead... Like the Paranoá Lake before me – crisp, rippled, and full of the most varied reflections.

My Taimbé is more here than in Taimbé itself: *in its inherent fluency, from Minas, / where the liquefying balconies, as lakes. / The cement of Brasília retains / the ways of an old plantation house...* I am a creeping vine poking into the soil in search of the new and creating hair roots with its head as it spreads. In the Pilot Plan, roots take flight and beat their wings like butterflies. Who can guarantee that I'm not artificial like Brasília? Taimbé is here, in my meeting Carlos. Minas is on the terrace of this house where Carlos and I are small town lovers. Where we are matters more than where we are going, or whence we have come.

When I tell Berenice that the Taimbé that interests me is all in my head and I don't want to ruin it, she doesn't understand. For her, it's as if she had never left Ceará, and Ceará is only there, it can never be anywhere else.

– Well, I miss my home, Dona Ana. You know, even Ipiranga, I still want to see before I die – she says.

One day she'll leave me yet, she'll return to Ceará.

In my case, without leaving here, I take the pulse of the Earth and learn how to surf the endless waves. I surf to keep my balance, to survive. The world spins and spins, and I'm not the one who's going to go chasing it. Carlos was the one who understood the wisdom of this slower rhythm.

I change nothing in his apartment except the chairs with the velvet covers, replaced by caned chairs. I feel good in this new beginning of life, more spare and economical. Carlos thinks I'm beautiful, he adores me, there's not a day that he doesn't bring me a gift, some simple thing, like another red rose from the garden, a symbol of love, which is a rose of many seasons. We sleep snuggled together in each other's arms, which sometimes arouses his desire in the early hours, and at these times a flower is also present, because he sees my genitals as a flower, a flower that in this season I feel is closed in its sincere shyness, but that opens, timid and dry, like the field flowers, for the devoted gardener who deflowers the trunk of my tree, branches rising in the dark. One night I have a nightmare and cry out apprehensive, I think someone in the room wants to kill me. Carlos reassures me; he makes me feel safe and secure.

Wanting happiness is to live with the anxiety of not achieving it. But it can arrive. What other name to give to what I feel, with Carlos surrounding me with attention? Loving what I have, not what's missing, I hear an echo of this happiness when I see Carlos, when I touch him, when I smell him or notice the expression on his face. I rest my anxiety on his loving shoulder. Love is a serene shared joy. We are kindred wanderers who have found and recognized each other. I'm starting from the end, with what the best marriages can aspire to after many years and much effort. Not to passion. To the possibility of friendship with tenderness, friendship open to desire. I love to love, and everything fits and will continue to fit inside the love that I feel, even the rages, sadnesses, and jealousies. In a little more than a year, how time has passed!

Nevertheless, I feel the emptiness Berta left, which will never be filled. Again I have the idea to write about the changes she provoked, with her arrival and departure. Without her, I would not have reconnected with some of my old friends over this past year, not even Cadu. Without her, I wouldn't have discovered true friendship, the friendship I'm trying to achieve more completely with Carlos. The disaster of her sudden brutal departure and its consequences were what led me to Carlos at last.

Rodolfo's absence pains me too. At least Lia and Josafá survived everything. They're with me even when they're not, because they run off to explore as always. It's the nature of cats. They were never domesticated by man, they're the ones who sought us for a congenial intimacy of mutual interest. Thus, Lia and Josafá sometimes visit me on the terrace, living freely in their cat world. Sometimes they walk through the charred house, they arrive covered in ashes.

I'm the one who can't even look over there without remembering that a piece of me is gone. We've decided that we're going to sell my lot and also Carlos' house and the two of us are going to move, to buy another house, here in Brasília, if possible also with a view of the lake. What I don't want is to see daily, toward the south, the location of my mistake.

Not everything in this place holds bad memories. Some days ago Carlos took me to the house balcony. After the rains, at last a clean landscape of uniform colors and defined features. A diurnal moon, almost full. Some birds flying over a very blue morning, a smooth lustrous blue, the kind that only exists here after the clouds fall from on high, washing the sky. Down below, roses of every color and above them, butterflies similar to those at the cemetery. Cheap poetry, crossed by my friend the rat who runs across the corner of the sidewalks, a homeless survivor. Carlos points to a small hole in the wall. There are two others like it, made by stray bullets, the ones I fired at the burglar who tried to invade my house.

And then he shows me the very bullets that he kept just because they came from my gun. I laugh, we laugh a lot, I like to laugh with Carlos, laughter connects us as it connected me to Eduardo one day, but now it will be different, Eduardo is pre-history, I'm more mature, time has mellowed me… Carlos kept the bullets as a souvenir of the night that he accompanied me home. From that night on, he tells me, I never left his mind. At that point he couldn't imagine that one day he would have me by his side. And, even when later he thought it possible, he almost gave up on me, he was certain that I wasn't interested in him, "but one shouldn't hang up his cleats just because he hasn't made a goal. The proof is that here we are today," he tells me while he wraps me in the muscles of his chest and kisses me tenderly.

Fate seems to want to make fun of us, but Carlos and I are determined to resist. First, a bill for six thousand reais arrives for Carlos to pay. He co-signed a loan Berta took out in Helena's name. It was undoubtedly the money she used to purchase her identity as Mona Habib. After Berta left my house, she begged him to sign the documents. She had no one else to ask, she was trying to make it on her own…

Another bill is the one from the boarding house where Berta was registered under Helena's name. To pay it, we took up a collection among the Useless. Berta's clothes, which I asked Berenice to distribute, and the folder with Helena's documents, were found there.

The worst is yet to happen and will shine more light on Berta's murder. It's ten-thirty on a night of clean air. The glow from the stars and the quarter moon dazzles me, increasing in intensity with every puff of the cigarettes that Cadu gave me. I smoke pot behind Carlos' back. Later I suggest we take a walk, remembering my strolls with Berta, she with her hands on her waist, wiggling for me and Vera, asking our advice about the right dose for her feminine gestures.

We, Carlos and I, walk to the edge of Lake Paranoá. I'm radiant and there's a moment when he takes me in his arms and we twirl, the world spinning in a carousel of joy. As we're arriving home, someone yells at me, pointing a gun:

– It's payback time, bitch!

I recognize the bastard I confronted that day. Carlos' muscles are good for something more than hugging me. He manages to grab the kid and twist his arm; he's forced to drop the weapon on the ground. Instinctively I pick it up, I try to aim at the son of a bitch, it's risky to fire, he and Carlos are struggling, he throws Carlos to the ground, I see Carlos stained with blood, the bastard comes at me, I warn him not to come close, he ignores me, keeps coming, then I fire the first shot, I hit him in the chest, I fire a second time, again I hit him, it's as if I were following the path of the bullet with all certainty, as if the bullet were under my control, I don't miss, the third shot hits him in the head, he falls, I fire a fourth, possibly fatal, at close range, again at his head, and at last, with the gun barrel at the motherfucker's ear, I replay my attempted suicide in a flashback and I fire one more, the last and fifth shot. Fortunately, Carlos had suffered only superficial wounds.

No one comes to see what happened. A longer than long, infinite absolute silence, as if there were no one in Brasília and it were the end of the world, the placid lake before us, streaked by the reflection of the lights and of the two of us before a bloody corpse. I'm tired of this reality that insists on invading my attempt at happiness alongside Carlos. I offer him the other joint, he doesn't want it, he doesn't care if I smoke it, and I do because I want to see things more clearly, to know what I ought to do… I see blood streaming from the wretch's head, there are no moral problems involved, I make a deep instantaneous examination of my conscience, and it's calmer than ever, as calm as the lake now, as calm as the starry sky, with that sliver of moon, stationary in its whiteness. In my internal settling of accounts, my soul is as clear as the air we are breathing tonight.

It's the moment to put my theory of instantaneism to the test. Analyzing the instant from all angles, I discern its crystalline shape. The way things appear now is the truth. It's as if the instant is physical and palpable, as if I can see it and touch it. In the instant everything becomes clear, as if I had found the perfect angle to connect all the facts of the story. I look at this instant and see with eyes open, as they have never been before. This is the city of the zero, the city of the void, I recall the conversation at the reunion of the Useless.

– He's still alive, the son of a bitch. He's laughing. I heard his laugh – I tell Carlos, a high metallic laugh that reverberated over the lake.

– No – Carlos answers.

– Yes, the son of a bitch is still alive.

– You're crazy, the guy is quite dead.

– No, I'm not crazy, I can see everything much more clearly, with a clarity that I haven't had in a long time, that in truth I never had – I say. The lake is a mirror, a true mirror, smooth, smooth, a blade of ice on which I can glide on skates. – When sound strikes the lake it jumps, reverberates into the air, amplifies and easily reaches our ears.

– I don't hear anything – says Carlos, who doesn't understand me because he's not stoned and doesn't have my clarity.

Then a wild fear gives me chills. Such fear and trembling will kill me; my heart will stop. My sweat turns cold, I'm pale, somewhat dizzy.

– It's low blood pressure – Carlos says.

I begin to cry, loudly, copiously, it's the end of me, it's the end of the world, I knew that everything would go wrong, the cretin stammered "You bitch, you'll pay dearly."

– The guy is dead – Carlos repeats, as if to calm me.

He puts me on the bed, covers me with a sheet, then brings salt, rubbing it on my lips.

– You'll feel better.

While I rest, he calls the police.

I didn't yet know that the gun I had fired at the son of a bitch was mine. Formiga had sold it to him or even given it to him, this I don't know for sure and it's secondary compared to the seriousness of his involvement with the bandit.

I haven't decided what to do about my nephew. For now, I think it's better that he stay there in Taimbé. I prefer not to reveal his whereabouts. I still believe that one day he'll be rehabilitated and become a good boy.

Yes, ever since the stories intersected, the police are after him and Pezão, who is in hiding. In tears, Berenice tells me that she dragged a confession from her son:

– Roberto Carlos isn't guilty.

For the first time I hear her call him by his real name.

It's too large a bomb for me to defuse! Perhaps Pezão himself, even Formiga, who knows, was behind the attempted robbery of my house. But what is this when faced with the monstrosity that at the very least they allowed to be committed?

I'm not going to judge anyone, I don't want to be a bitch. I can't escape it, I'm a bitch one way or another; if I turn in Formiga and also if I lie. I can, however, avoid being a bitch to the second power. I'm not going to protect Formiga and incriminate Pezão. The two deserve each other, they're worth the same, one worse than the other. No, actually Pezão's worth more, at least he tries to get a job, Formiga never did anything in his life.

– It's my fault – I tell Chicão. – I'm the one who didn't know how to raise him. I took the easy way out. Because I wanted to seem liberal-minded.

– No. You're not responsible for what he does. He's an adult, he knows his own mind. Look at Vera. She's a well brought up girl – he says, without knowing the problems I've had with her. – And you gave the two of them the same upbringing.

I now have a new version of instantaneism, less skeptical and less relativist. I still believe that reality is the present instant, but what present exists without the pain of absence? The instant itself collects what remained, resurrects what died, makes predictions and, there in a corner, lets a tiny star shine, a stubborn surviving flame that is no more than a serene attitude before fate. I became a skeptic on skepticism, a pessimist about pessimism. Instead of having hope, I keep trying, I don't abdicate the effort of finding a beautiful garment for uncertainty. Chicão's gift – Our Lady of Hope – reposes, by the way, on a shelf in the living room, next to the Chinese figurine that Berta gave me.

I'm not composing a story here from the words I salvaged, or from the ones I eliminated or the ones that I wrote to replace those I was discarding. What is essential isn't found in the diary that I destroyed or in the story that I later lost in the catastrophe, but rather in what I relate now. This, my monologue, is truer, not just because it's more spontaneous. Wisdom decants at the same pace, as the words that carry it on the river of time are constantly changing their surroundings until they settle in the ocean depths.

With the words I'm gathering here, I salvage the spirit of my story, which was just one wish: the wish to say what I think at the instant I think it, with the story being simply the reality of this instant, nothing more. This story is definitive not because it replaces all the others, as I had once hoped, but because it is fragile; when it ends, this story is entirely the past of this instant and can be kept intact, like a painting, forever. Like the afternoon outside, like the sun that enters through the window, like Carlos' presence. There will never be another moment like it. This is an unexpected instant of my writing to which I devote myself entirely. Diana guides me. She loosens my tied tongue, releases my speech in the ink of this anxious pen. She is determined, arbitrary. She hates silence. She lives in the noise of the world, the opposite of me. She connects sentences, meanings, without mincing words.

The definitive text, living and unique, that sums up everything and that is the present instant, cannot be a zero. It is everything, a totality that remakes itself totally, that omits nothing, that incorporates what can be recalled, although it allows forgetting; that exists in the chaos of noise and the silent spaces. It's a hypertext that recreates itself at every instant with words whispered by God that become lost in the midst of the ashes and are only found after much effort.

I don't doubt that I will yet live a long time. My portrait as an old woman, the only one of my few objects that is with me, acquired a patina of smoke, a diaphanous transparency that diminished my wrinkles and erased the gap that separated Ana from Diana. My face is transformed when I look at this painting. The years have drawn many folds on my face, not the same ones that Norberto painted; others, created with more depth and bitterness. But suddenly, I feel lighter and younger. At last, I am my true self, stripped of the impurities, excesses, and the weight of years. My masks have dropped. I realize what happened: Diana's image merged with Ana's, producing this new painting. Despite everything I have suffered and still suffer, I am reborn, not from zero, because I have discovered that even a new life doesn't begin from zero. But the old in it is rejuvenated. I'm also what I was and what I no longer am.

I look behind the picture: the fire destroyed the paper that I glued here, the sheet with the dream I had decades ago about Cadu. Carbonized traces of desire remain. I caress them with my hands that blacken with ash. Then I rub my hands on my face, so that the ash can penetrate my wrinkles, as I did on the day I visited the remains of my house. Carlos will think it strange to see me with this black mask, neither Ana nor Diana.

I survived the hedonism of my youth and the chastity of my maturity, my heroic egoism, my lack of money and happiness, my depression. I'm determined to live much longer.

Carlos is right, life is like a soccer game, only with many different goal posts. You have to try to score in every one. Never quit. Or perhaps there is no goal, only a circular field where we dribble past our opponents, the devils who make our lives hell, in order to go on living. I'm a castaway he saved and brought to safe harbor, with my cats and Berenice. Or is this a fairy tale? Sometimes I fear that I abandon one illusion for another, and then I think about the terrible dream where Carlos appeared as the police officer who came to arrest me.

It's a passing fear. Carlos is more than Paulinho; he's not a childhood dream. He's not perfect like the idealized recreations of the past or the best faces of the future. He's the one I have now, with the imperfections that every present contains. He's the one who not just in spirit, but in flesh and blood, fills the emptiness of this prolonged instant that I describe. I want a Carlos whom I won't have to miss, the Carlos against whom not even death, or anguish, or nothingness has power; who is indestructible and eternal. Despite death. Despite time. It must be because love didn't come to me, rather I went to it.

Pezão is jailed. Berenice tells me that he hardly knew the two guys who had followed Berta when she left the club, at first it only looked like a joke. Pezão and Formiga had tried to prevent the crime, carried out only by the other two. One of them was Fefé, the jailed thug. The other was even more dangerous and had threatened to kill Pezão – it's a good thing I had carried out justice, killing him. Formiga had witnessed everything, "and witnessing isn't a crime, Miss Ana"; Pezão hadn't even done that much, he had fled well before.

Better to cover my ears. Mostly I don't want to hear that Berta was stabbed with scissors. More than sixty times. Why doesn't Berenice spare me these details? Why would I want to know that the thug I killed had commented that he was going "to spill the stiff's guts in a ditch"? Those vermin, Berenice says, had suggested more than once getting Berta as she left the club, the idea hadn't been Pezão's or Formiga's, no way.

– My son made a mistake, but he's no criminal – she repeats to me – and you can be sure Ma'am, that he's not going to rat on Formiga.

– I love you – Carlos says as he comforts me with a hug, and I am moved by these simple words that I hadn't heard in so long.

– I love you, too – I reply sincerely.

I want what's absolutely simple, that soothes me, a peaceful gaze over my chosen city, a stroll along the edge of Lake Paranoá that I suggest now to Carlos.

Cities change over time, as they become familiar. I no longer feel like a stranger in Brasília. I have new eyes and a new heart for the unchanging landscapes. The city no longer frightens me, and the hopes that it generates, in spite of myself, are within my grasp. The city is mine, with its empty spaces, its coldness, and its solitude. I have become intimate with its dry dusty air, the uniformity of its residential blocks, its long axes under the giant sky.

The city of the d's, as they say, is no longer the city of dazzle, of disappointment, of despair, the city of my divorce. It's not the city of dementia. I'm not demented just because I like this city again. Brasília ceased being my voluntary prison. It's the city of Diana, huntress of illusions; of lost dreams among landscapes of desolation. Because I love to love, I want to live in this space where the vision of the future was preserved among fossils and the artifices of this new millennium. Building a city from nothing is a bet on life. I want to live on the frontier that advances across the immense emptiness. To rebuild myself out of the ashes.

I'm in a state of grace facing destiny, perhaps because of the new autumn that I see in the violet blue of the jacarandas, or because Carlos already awaits me on the terrace of our house, ready for our stroll. I want to receive the hot sun on my face. To become drunk on the excess of light that projects a shadow of dreams. My temporary pains, if they are on the one hand so terrible and cruel, are curing another insistent annoying migraine-like pain, the pain of my daily tragedy.

I see the immense sky before me, there on the other side of the lake, above the ministry buildings, where an enormous red sun blinds me. I remember the day after receiving Berta's letter when I was driving along the Grand Axis, on the way to Chicão's apartment. The sky that I saw that day was like this one. The same cloud of questioning rises, this time even redder and reflected in the lake.

It has been a little more than a year. I remember Norberto's letter, Carlos' face when he offered me a flower on that hot afternoon, the revolver I carried in my purse, a horrifying bloody dream. After discovering that the instant is not a uniform measure of time, I decide to transport myself to that crucial instant, to climb onto it, to allow myself to be freely carried by it, and to describe it in a continuous present, like a security camera never independent of me.